Classical Literature: A Very Short Introduction

VERY SHORT INTRODUCTIONS are for anyone wanting a stimulating and accessible way into a new subject. They are written by experts, and have been translated into more than 45 different languages.

The series began in 1995, and now covers a wide variety of topics in every discipline. The VSI library now contains over 500 volumes—a Very Short Introduction to everything from Psychology and Philosophy of Science to American History and Relativity—and continues to grow in every subject area.

Titles in the series include the following:

William Allan

CLASSICAL LITERATURE

A Very Short Introduction

OXFORD
UNIVERSITY PRESS

OXFORD
UNIVERSITY PRESS

Great Clarendon Street, Oxford, OX2 6DP,
United Kingdom

Oxford University Press is a department of the University of Oxford.
It furthers the University's objective of excellence in research, scholarship,
and education by publishing worldwide. Oxford is a registered trade mark of
Oxford University Press in the UK and in certain other countries

© William Allan 2014

The moral rights of the author have been asserted

First Edition published in 2014
Impression: 9

Published in the United States of America by Oxford University Press
198 Madison Avenue, New York, NY 10016, United States of America

British Library Cataloguing in Publication Data
Data available

Library of Congress Control Number: 2013953491

ISBN 978-0-19-966545-7

Printed in Great Britain by
Ashford Colour Press Ltd, Gosport, Hampshire

For Penny, Brian, and Russell

Contents

Preface

A very short introduction deserves a very short preface. I am grateful to Andrea Keegan and Emma Ma, Senior and Senior Assistant Commissioning Editors of the VSI series, for their help throughout. The book was written in the splendidly renovated reading room of the Staatsbibliothek zu Berlin (Unter den Linden), and I am indebted to the staff there for their friendly assistance. I would also like to thank Mike Squire and Chris Whitton for help with illustrations and for many happy memories of life in Berlin. Finally, my wife Laura Swift read the book carefully and improved it in countless ways and I am hugely grateful to her as always.

W. R. A.
Berlin
July 2013

List of illustrations

List of maps

Chapter 1
History, genre, text

To give a brief overview of the history of classical literature, a period spanning over 1,200 years (*c.*750 BC to AD 500), might appear to be the work of a madman. In comparison, the contestants in *Monty Python*'s 'All-England Summarize Proust Competition' had a whole 15 seconds to sum up just seven novels. But an attempt must be made nonetheless, since a sketch of the terrain will come in handy in future chapters, where we look in more detail at the major genres of classical literature.

The conventional periodization of classical literature—broadly speaking, archaic, classical, Hellenistic, and imperial for Greek literature; Republican and imperial for Latin (we'll come back to these divisions later)—mirrors the familiar chunks of ancient history. It is not unusual for literary and historical periodization to go together in the study of a particular literature (English, French, German, and so on), since most people accept that we can trace historical change through literature.

Of course, all such periodizations are artificial constructions, created by scholars after the event. In reality one can't draw a neat dividing line between literary or historical periods, since they flow into one another. But with certain caveats in place—that is, as long as we take care not to obscure the continuities between periods, or suggest that there was little change within a specific era, or reduce the meaning of a particular text to its expression of a supposedly 'archaic' or 'Neronian' (etc.) worldview—the customary division into periods can be useful. After all, literary forms do evolve over time and are linked to wider political and cultural changes, so some effort to trace these developments and define particular phases is both desirable and appropriate.

As well as acting as helpful signposts in a large expanse of time, literary historical terms can also point to meaningful differences in central themes and concerns between periods—compare, for example, the varying preoccupations suggested by 'Romanticism' or 'Victorian' in English literature. The scholar's job is made easier when the birth of a new literary movement is proclaimed by the writers themselves, as when the third-century BC Greek poet Callimachus presents a manifesto of erudite and recherché literature, inaugurating what is often called the 'Hellenistic' or 'Alexandrian' aesthetic. But even when writers are not so self-conscious, we can trace in retrospect the emergence of distinct movements, even if the alleged break with the past is often exaggerated, whether by the writers themselves or later critics: Virginia Woolf's playful comment, 'On or about December 1910 human character changed' ('Mr Bennet and Mrs Brown', 1924), well expresses both the temptation and the danger of discerning sharp breaks between eras.

Any outline of classical literary periods will feel at times like a crash course in ancient history, but I prefer to think of that as a good thing: after all, literature always has its roots in the reality of its times, even when it goes beyond them. Thus ancient fantasy fiction (see Chapter 9) reflects in a topsy-turvy fashion the limits of ancient knowledge of the world, just as modern science fiction has engaged with technological and political developments for well over a century. Great works of literature may be in some sense 'timeless', but one cannot fully understand classical (or any other) literature without some knowledge of its original historical context.

The collapse of Mycenaean culture around 1200 BC was followed by several centuries of Greek history in which the skill of writing was unknown, but oral poetry and story-telling of various kinds flourished. In the early 8th century BC the Greeks adapted the Phoenician alphabet to suit their own language, and the tradition of Greek 'literature' (i.e. a record of written texts) begins. By a fluke of history the rediscovery of writing coincided with the genius of Homer, so that his great epics, the *Iliad* and *Odyssey*, composed around 725–700 BC, are not only the greatest works of classical literature but also the earliest (imagine English literature beginning, Big Bang style, with Shakespeare). The period from the first Olympic Games in 776 BC to the end of the Persian Wars in 479 BC is conventionally known as the Archaic age, but the word 'archaic' should not be taken to imply 'primitive', since this is one of the most dynamic and experimental periods of Greek literature, and the epic and lyric poetry that survives is among the most impressive and sophisticated ever written (see Chapters 2 and 3). The archaic age was also a period of expansion and colonization, as Greek cities sent out traders and settlers all around the Mediterranean, ranging from Massalia (modern Marseille) to Naucratis in Egypt (over 50 miles down the Nile), and this cultural energy and diversity is reflected in the major writers of the period, who come from all corners of the Greek-speaking world (see Map 1).

By contrast, the literature of the Classical period (479–323 BC), from the defeat of Persia to the death of Alexander the Great, is dominated by one city above all, Athens. The Greeks' victory over the huge Persian invading force not only bolstered their sense of superiority to 'barbarians' (non-Greeks), but also allowed the Athenians to exploit an originally defensive alliance (the Delian League, formed to repel further Persian attacks) for their own ends, turning it into the engine of an Athenian empire. The wealth of empire, combined with an open democratic culture, attracted intellectuals and artists from all over the Greek world, making Athens the cultural centre of Greece, 'the school of Hellas', as

Map 1. The Greek world

4

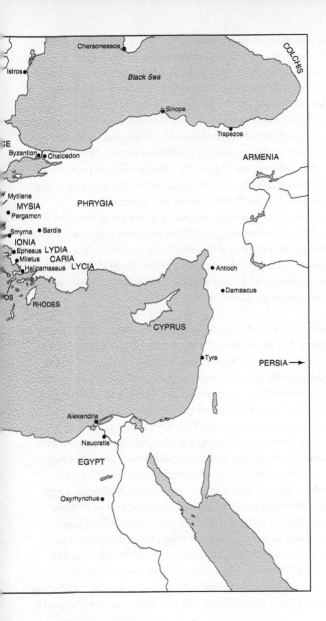

Pericles calls it in his eulogy of the city (Thucydides, *History* 2.41). Literary forms flourished around the public performance spaces of Athenian democracy: tragedy and comedy at the state-sponsored dramatic festivals (Chapter 4), oratory in the law-courts and assembly (Chapter 6), and historiography in the circles of politicians and intellectuals who were interested in understanding (among other things) why Greece had been successful in the Persian Wars or why Athens lost the Peloponnesian War against Sparta (431–404 BC; see Chapter 5). Athens' cultural importance survived its defeat by Sparta at the end of the fifth century, as did its democracy, and the fourth century saw a continued efflorescence of great writing, especially in the prose forms of oratory, history, and philosophy (little poetry has survived). As with 'archaic' literature, it is important not to confuse 'classical' with 'safe' or 'bland': the best authors of the classical period are truly revolutionary and influenced the major forms of drama, poetry, and prose for centuries to come.

The Hellenistic period (323–31 BC), from the death of Alexander the Great to Octavian's defeat of Mark Antony and Cleopatra VII of Egypt at the battle of Actium, saw a huge expansion of Greek (and subsequently Greco-Roman) culture. Alexander's campaigns had taken him as far as the Persian Gulf, India, and Afghanistan, and his generals inherited a variety of successor kingdoms, the most enduring being that of the Ptolemies in Egypt. Ptolemy I founded the Library and Museum at Alexandria, the former with the ambition of collecting and cataloguing every Greek literary text ever written, the latter as a research centre for scholars in every field of the arts and sciences. Subsequent Ptolemaic kings continued their patronage of both institutions, and in such an ostentatiously learned, and blissfully subsidized, milieu there emerged a new literary movement which fused literature and scholarship as never before. The hallmarks of the 'Alexandrian' style are erudition and refinement. Its guru, the scholar-poet Callimachus, proclaimed 'I sing nothing that is unattested'. Earlier literature had also been allusive and inventive, but now the poet's learning became much more overt and self-conscious, and innovation even more prized. While some authors get mired in wearisome obscurity and self-defeating cleverness (Nicander's poems on various kinds of poison and their antidotes, for example, are enough by themselves to make the blood run cold), the best writers of the period use their learning to revive hackneyed literary forms (as in Callimachus' and Apollonius' transformations of epic: Chapter 2) or to create ingenious new ones (Theocritus' invention of pastoral: Chapter 7).

Thus far our focus has been on Greek literature. Though Rome was founded (according to ancient reckoning) in 753 BC, no trace of Latin literature has survived before the mid-third century BC. Thus the first few centuries of the Republican period (509–31 BC), from the expulsion of the last Roman king, Tarquinius Superbus, and the proclamation of a republican system of government down to that system's self-destruction in the civil wars of the first century BC, are in literary terms a blank page. But the earliest surviving Latin literature—the epics of Livius Andronicus, Naevius, and Ennius, the tragedies of Ennius and Pacuvius, and the comedies of Plautus and Terence (these last being the only early texts to survive complete)—shows that, as with 'archaic' Greek literature, we should beware of confusing 'early' with 'unsophisticated'. For these works, composed around 240–130 BC, not only reflect on the Romans' stupendous military successes during this period, which made Rome the major power in the Mediterranean world, but also engage with their Greek literary models in a highly ambitious and creative manner. Ennius, for example, presented himself as the reincarnation of Homer, the ultimate symbol of Greek culture's transference to Rome (Chapter 2).

By adapting Greek literary forms to suit new audiences and concerns, and by combining them with native Italian traditions, these early writers begin the process, continued by all subsequent Latin authors, of 'making it Roman'. When Greece itself came under Roman domination in 146 BC, the influence of Greek literature and culture on Rome grew even stronger, and one contemporary politician and writer, the elder Cato, took advantage of popular anxiety surrounding such aristocratic philhellenism by constructing in opposition to it a persona of no-nonsense, back-to-basics Roman simplicity. (Cato's writings show him to be well read in Greek literature, but he realized there was political mileage in appealing to Roman contempt for arty-farty Greeks, who were now also their provincial subjects.) Most Latin authors, however, were more open about their debt to the Greek tradition. The intensity of this cultural interaction is best expressed in Horace's intentionally paradoxical observation: 'Greece, once captured, made a captive of her wild conqueror/and introduced the arts to rustic Latium' (Horace, *Epistles* 2.1.156–7). In other words, Rome's military expansion led to cultural enrichment as well. The centre of literary creativity (first Athens, then Alexandria) was now Rome. Though no major Latin author of the Republican period was born in Rome, they all made their way there in search of patronage, audiences, and success.

In the last decades of the republic greed and self-interest destroyed the welfare of the state, as warlords like Caesar and Pompey, Octavian and Mark Antony, deployed unprecedented violence against their fellow citizens. The literature of the period struggles to make sense of the chaos, and there are scathing attacks on political ambition in Lucretius, Catullus, and Sallust. Many of the greatest figures in Latin literature lived through the republic's collapse into dictatorship, and their works (especially those of Cicero, Virgil, and Horace) offer profound explorations not only of the impact of civil war, but also of the imperial system that the civil wars gave birth to (see Chapters 2, 3, and 6). Octavian (63 BC–AD 14) secured sole power at the battle of Actium in 31 BC and took the title 'Augustus' (connoting religious and political authority) in 27 BC, becoming the first emperor and implementing an imperial system whose revolutionary and tyrannical nature he cleverly sought to disguise by proclaiming himself the restorer of the republic.

The Augustan age (44 BC–AD 17), from the assassination of Julius Caesar (and the emergence of his 19-year-old heir, Octavian) until the death of the poet Ovid, spans the violent transition from republic to empire, and its outstanding authors (Virgil, Horace, Tibullus, Propertius, Ovid, and Livy) articulate the relationship between literature and power with remarkable insight, and it is their at times troubling reflections on the recent past which give their work its edge. Naturally, each of these writers reacts to the new regime in his own way, and their responses develop over time, as the imperial system itself evolves, so there is no one 'Augustan' literature. Thus there is a world of difference between the early works of Virgil and Horace from the 30s BC, when Roman society was still tearing itself apart and no end or clear victor was in sight, and the works of Ovid, written from around 16 BC onwards, in which Augustus and his power are facts of life.

The Augustan poets strive to match the Greek classics: Virgil claims the mantle of Homer, Horace is the new Alcaeus (not to mention every other Greek lyric poet), and Propertius claims to be the new Callimachus. As with the term 'classical', however, the sense of 'Augustan' (as a period in English literature) meaning 'measured' or 'harmonious' risks obscuring the revolutionary nature of these works. Indeed the daring and ambition of these writers are most clearly seen in the ways they engage with Augustus' transformation of Roman society itself, including at times their refusal to celebrate it (Chapter 3).

Such is the quality of the literature written in the late Republican and Augustan eras that it is traditionally known as the Golden Age of Latin literature, followed by the Silver Age of the early empire (AD 17–130). But such terms, with their evaluative connotations, are no longer fashionable, and in any case they undervalue the success of many imperial writers in adapting to new circumstances: the epic poet Lucan, the novelist Petronius, the satirist Juvenal, and the historian Tacitus are a match for any before them. Not surprisingly a central concern of all imperial

Latin literature is the relationship between the writer and the emperor, as well as the writer's relationship to the literary past. Augustus exiled Ovid to the Black Sea in AD 8 and banned his saucy love poetry from his library on the Palatine, Tiberius (who reigned 14–37) forced the pro-republican historian Cremutius Cordus to commit suicide and burnt his books, while Nero (54–68) had Lucan, Petronius, and Seneca (his own former tutor and adviser) all kill themselves. Domitian (81–96) was particularly paranoid and despotic, and he is attacked by Tacitus, Pliny, and Juvenal—but from a safe distance, after the emperor is dead and his dynasty finished. It is easy for us to look down on the sycophancy of writers like Statius and Pliny, with their panegyrics of reigning emperors; conformity is never as sexy as rebellion. But their decision to work within the system is understandable, and makes Lucan's anti-imperial polemics and Tacitus' mordant analysis of Roman history since Augustus all the more impressive.

Greek literature of the imperial period is marked by a similar concern with the power of Rome (cf. Map 2). The philhellenism of Roman emperors like Hadrian (117–38) and Marcus Aurelius (161–80) encouraged a renaissance of Greek literature under Roman patronage, as Romans of the governing class were keen to associate themselves with the prestige of Greek culture and educated Greeks were only too happy to broker it to them. Although much of the Greek literature that survives from the imperial period is marred by an artificial classicism and a romanticizing approach to the good old days of Greek self-government, the best writers break free of such stultifying nostalgia and present more creative responses to Roman power and Latin literature. The *Parallel Lives* of Plutarch, for example, where the biography of an eminent Greek is paired with that of a Roman whose life shows points of resemblance in both virtue and in vice (Alexander the Great with Julius Caesar, Demosthenes with Cicero, and so on), breaks down cultural stereotypes on both sides, reminding the Romans that the Greeks can be great warriors and statesmen and not simply decadent aesthetes, and

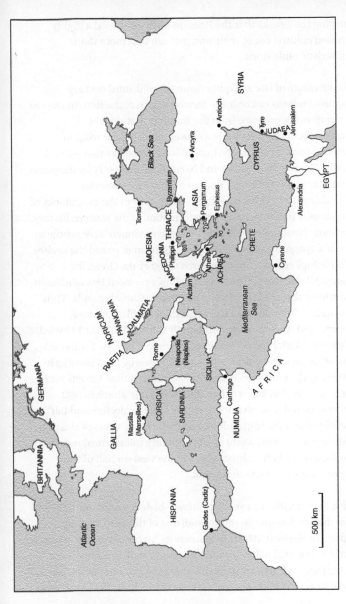

Map 2. The Roman Empire in the time of Augustus

showing the Greeks that the Romans have developed a highly civilized cultural life of their own and are thus more than militaristic philistines.

The literature of late antiquity (from the mid-third century onwards) reflects not only the fragmentation of the Roman empire under growing pressure from the frontiers, but also the establishment of Christianity as the empire's official religion. Classical literature of a high quality is still being created—Greek epic by Quintus Smyrnaeus and Nonnus, Latin poetry by Ausonius, Claudian, and Prudentius, Roman history by Ammianus Marcellinus (a Greek, but writing in Latin)—but the ascendancy of Christianity marks a crucial transformation of the western literary tradition. Nonetheless, although many churchmen were hostile to classical (pagan) culture—'The same lips cannot sound the praises of both Jupiter and Christ', declared Gregory the Great, for example—classical culture was not simply replaced by Christianity, but widely absorbed into it, and adapted to Christian ends. Thus the works of foundational Christian thinkers like Ambrose, Jerome, and Augustine are profoundly indebted to their knowledge of classical literature. So while various events may vie for the title 'end of the classical world'—the sack of Rome by the Visigoths in 410 being the most iconic, since it was the first time the city had been taken by foreign invaders since the Gauls' attack in 390 BC—we should take care not to let the familiar 'decline and fall' model obscure the continuities, especially in the study of classical texts, as the classical world of late antiquity transformed itself into the societies of Latin Christendom in the western half of the empire and Byzantium in the east.

With these 1,200 or so years of literary history under our belt, it is now time to consider in more detail one of the most striking aspects of classical literature, namely its highly developed sense of genre. Obviously, a literary work's genre remains an important factor today: we too distinguish broad categories of poetry, prose, and drama, but also sub-genres (especially within the novel, now the most popular literary form) such as crime, romantic, or historical fiction. And we do the same in other creative media, such as film, with thrillers, horrors, westerns, and so on. But classical authors were arguably even more aware than writers of genre fiction are today what forms and conventions applied to the genre they were writing in. All ancient literary texts are written in a particular genre, even when they are also interacting with others—as in 'tragic history', for example, that is history written in the style of tragedy. Some modern theorists would argue that every text belongs to a genre and that it is impossible not to write in one: thus even those writers who try to break free of convention and write the wackiest stuff are still caught up in 'experimental' literature. The invention of the major literary genres and their norms is the most significant effect of classical literature's influence. Accordingly, this introduction too is structured primarily by genre, reflecting its importance.

But what is a genre? The first thing to observe is that a genre is *not* a timeless and unchanging Platonic form, but a group of texts that share certain similarities—whether of form, performance context, or subject matter—and present a continuous development of these similarities over time. For example, all the texts that make up the ancient genre of tragedy share certain 'family resemblances' (they are theatrical texts written in a particular poetic language, they reflect on human suffering, they show gods interacting with humans, and so on) that allow us to perceive them as a recognizable group. But although certain 'core' features characterize any given genre, the boundaries of each genre are fluid and are often breached for literary effect.

As can still be seen in modern literature and film, a genre comes with certain in-built codes, values, and expectations. It creates its own world, helping the author to communicate with the audience, as she deploys or disrupts generic expectations and so creates a variety of effects. Genres appeal to writers because they give a structure and something to build on, while they offer audiences

13

the pleasure of the familiar and ingenious diversion from it. The best writers take what they need from the traditional form and then innovate, leaving their own imprint on the genre and changing it for future writers and audiences. In other words, genre is a source of dynamism and creativity, not a straitjacket, unless the writer is unimaginative or unoriginal.

All ancient writers had an idea of who the top figures in their chosen genre were, and their aim was to rival and outdo their predecessors. The key ancient terms for this process of interaction with the literary past are *imitatio* ('imitation') and *aemulatio* ('competition'). 'Imitation' does not mean slavish copying, but creative adaptation of the tradition; creative writing today still involves the reworking of previous literature, since writers are usually enthusiastic readers too. Of course, competing with the great writers of the past is a risky business—as Horace puts it, 'Whoever strives to rival Pindar exposes himself to a flight as risky as that of Icarus' (*Odes* 4.2.1-4, paraphrased)—but what characterizes the best writers of antiquity is their response to the great works of the past in the light of the present.

Classical literature is characterized by a hierarchy of genres, ranging from 'high' forms such as epic, tragedy, and history at one end through to 'low' forms such as comedy, satire, mime, and epigram at the other. 'High' and 'low' relate to how serious the subject matter is, how lofty the language, how diginified the tone, and so on. Many of the genres lower down on the hierarchy define themselves polemically in opposition to a higher form: thus writers of comedy, for example, poke fun at tragedy, presenting it as unrealistic and bombastic, in order to assert the value of their own work, while satire mocks the claims of epic and philosophy (among other genres) to offer meaningful guides to life. Finally, it is striking that some genres endure longer than others: Roman love elegy flourished for only half a century (see Chapter 3), while epic was always there, and always changing (Chapter 2). In conclusion, then, we can understand an ancient literary text

14

properly only if we take into account where it comes in the evolution of its genre, and how it engages with and transforms the conventions it inherits.

Let us end this introductory chapter by considering how it is we have the classical texts we do. The vast majority (at least 90 per cent) of classical literature is lost: so, for example, from the (at least) 900 tragedies produced during the 5th century BC at the major annual dramatic festival in Athens only 31 have survived intact, i.e. little more than 3 per cent of the most prestigious and popular genre of classical Athens. Some losses are more serious than others: few will lose much sleep over the fact that Dio Chrysostom's eulogies on a parrot and a gnat have not made the cut. And the vagaries of survival are cruel: we have only seven tragedies of Sophocles (from an oeuvre of over 120 plays), but no less than 1,600 letters of Libanius, a Greek rhetorician of the 4th century AD, proof (if any were needed) that the universe is random and life unfair.

Ancient texts, complete and fragmentary, come down to us either in an unbroken succession of copies (a manuscript tradition) or on ancient papyri which have been excavated in recent times. Like all texts until the invention of the printing press in the 15th century, classical texts were copied by hand, by skilled scribes (usually slaves), who did their best to produce an exact copy of their 'orginal'. But errors naturally entered the text as it was copied and recopied, especially because ancient texts, with no word-division and almost no punctuation, were much harder to read than modern texts, especially printed ones. One task of the classical scholar is to spot these errors and undo them.

The survival of classical literature is therefore the story of a very long and gradual process of selection and narrowing, as fewer and fewer texts were read and recopied. A number of factors contributed to this process, some deliberate, some accidental. Among the former the most important were: selection for use in the school curriculum (if a text was deemed, for example, too difficult linguistically or too naughty, it was in trouble); the reliance on anthologies, or collections of 'highlights' (like modern Dictionaries of Quotations), which led to the loss of complete works; the influence of scholarly 'canons', that is, lists of the 'best' authors in each genre, such as the Nine Lyric Poets or the Three Great Tragedians, which also influenced the choice of texts used in schools; and finally, and most intangibly of all, the influence of public taste and the perception of quality, for as Horace says, 'the existence of mediocre poets/neither men nor gods nor booksellers will accept' (*Art of Poetry* 372–3). Other factors had nothing to do with the nature of the literature involved: nibbling bookworms, mould, and the destruction of libraries by fire, as when the great Library of Alexandria, with its half a million papyrus rolls, burnt to the ground during Julius Caesar's attack on the city in 48 BC.

Further bottlenecks intervened, such as the change in the physical shape of the text, from the papyrus roll to the more practical codex, a form akin to our modern book. This transition, which began in the late 1st century AD and was largely complete by the end of the 4th, meant that only those works recopied into the new format had a fair chance of surviving. The codex format was particularly favoured by Christians, which brings us to our final hurdle, namely Christian censorship and neglect. We should take care, however, not to be too hard on the Christians, since they did recognize the quality of pagan texts and came up with ingenious ways of making them acceptable: for example, by allegorizing them in Christian terms, as when Virgil's fourth *Eclogue* was read as a harbinger of the birth of Christ (see Chapter 7). And it is to the monastic and cathedral libraries throughout medieval Christendom, as well as to Islamic philosophers and scholars of this period, that we owe the preservation of the texts themselves, until their rediscovery in, and ignition of, the Renaissance.

Fortunately, some of the accidents of history are happy ones, and new classical texts, often preserved as papyrus fragments in the

1. A papyrus from Oxyrhynchus in Egypt, discovered in 1897 and first published in 2005. The text is by the 7th-century BC poet Archilochus and narrates the Greeks' first campaign against Troy, which badly misfires when they attack another city by mistake and are defeated by its king, Telephus

rubbish mounds of Egypt, are still being discovered and published: thus the last few years have seen the publication of previously unknown works by two of the greatest Greek lyric poets, Sappho and Archilochus (first editions in 2004 and 2005, respectively: see Figure 1). And new technologies, such as multi-spectral imaging, have made it possible to read texts that before were illegible, such as those written on charred rolls of papyrus, carbonized by the eruption of Mt Vesuvius in AD 79. New discoveries and new approaches of this kind continue to transform our view of classical literature.

Chapter 2
Epic

Epic was not only the most prestigious but also the most malleable and enduring of ancient literary forms. The classical world was full of war, whether between rival Greek city-states or between Rome and those who dared to resist the expansion of her dominion: the gates of Janus in Rome were closed only in times of complete peace, and when Caesar's heir (the future Augustus) closed them in 29 BC, it was the first time in 200 years and only the third time in seven centuries of Roman history. In societies where warfare was endemic, a genre which both celebrated and explored such concepts as military heroism, loyalty, and masculinity would never lose its relevance or popularity.

In the skill of their narrative and characterization, their use of language, and the richness of their imaginative world, Homer's *Iliad* and *Odyssey* are the supreme works of classical literature. They burst like miracles from the gloomy 'dark ages' of Greece (the period from around 1200 to 776 BC, following the collapse of Mycenaean culture) and their importance for the shaping of later Greco-Roman culture is unmatched. In an ancient version of *Desert Island Discs*, it would be Homer's epics, the classical equivalent of the Bible and Shakespeare, which would be pre-packed for the journey. Western literature seems to begin with a double paradox: Homer's works are the earliest but also the best, and Homer himself is arguably the greatest poet who ever lived and yet we know nothing about him. But neither issue is really a problem: the *Iliad* and *Odyssey* may be the earliest Greek literature to survive, but they are in fact the culmination of a centuries-old tradition of oral epic poetry, while our ignorance of Homer's identity is irrelevant to our appreciation of his poetry.

Like nearly all classical epic, Homer's tales of the Trojan War and Odysseus' return to Ithaca are set in the mythical world of gods and heroes. There is likely to be a historical core to the Greek epic tradition and its account of the fall of Troy—that is, some reminiscence of a Greek attack on north-western Asia Minor (modern Turkey) in the early 12th century BC—but when history becomes heroic poetry it inevitably becomes a form of fiction. By the time of Homer in the late 8th century BC many generations of bards had transformed the story of the Trojan War to suit the needs of successive eras and audiences. What was originally a conflict fought for complex military and political reasons becomes a war fought for a woman (Helen of Troy), and poetic exaggeration has left its mark: ten years of fighting, an armada of 1,186 Greek ships, and so on. Most striking is the Homeric poems' nostalgia for a bygone Heroic Age, which becomes a leitmotif of the epic tradition, as seen, for example, in the Homeric warriors' physical superiority to men of today: 'A man could not easily lift that rock with both hands, even a very strong man, such as mortals now are' (*Iliad* 12.381–3).

To appreciate Homer's achievement, we must first consider the oral epic tradition that he inherited. Homer composed for live performance, and even if he was literate (we do not know this for sure), he learned his craft from other performing bards. He will have perfected his poems over many years, usually delivering short episodes rather than the entire work (it would take around 26 hours to perform the entire *Iliad*). Like any other itinerant artist, keen to drum up future patronage, Homer takes care to advertise his own skill: the bard Phemius in the *Odyssey* asserts that such skill comes through hard practice as well as divine inspiration:

'I am self-taught, and god has put in my mind every pathway of song' (22.347–8). And it is no coincidence that the central heroes of both epics, Achilles and Odysseus, are compared to epic poets, as when Odysseus stringing his bow is likened to a bard stringing his lyre (*Odyssey* 21.406–11).

Despite its great size (almost 16,000 lines of poetry), the *Iliad* covers only a short period in the Trojan War, concentrating on just four days of fighting from the tenth and final year. As Aristotle observed (*Poetics* ch. 23), Homer avoids the mistake made by some later epic poets, who tried to cover every episode in their chosen myth from start to finish, leading merely to a dull sequence of events ('*a* happened, and then *b*, and then…'). Instead Homer chose a single, unified action within the story of Troy's fall (the anger of Achilles) and expanded it, using flashbacks and foreshadowings, so that his narrative embraces the entire war, ranging from Helen's original abduction by the Trojan prince Paris (the cause of the Greek expedition) through to the destruction of Troy and the enslavement of its surviving population. This skilful use of time (past, present, and future) is one of the best examples of the *Iliad*'s careful and sophisticated structure.

We refer to the main figures of Homeric epic as heroes, but it is important that we make clear what being a 'hero' means in this context. For us the term 'hero' conjures up someone who has done something unambiguously positive: a fireman who rushes into a burning building to save people, for example. In ancient Greek culture, however, the 'heroes', the offspring of unions between gods and humans, are not simply positive figures, but are characterized by their excessiveness, both for good and for ill. The heroes are capable of acts of superhuman and admirable prowess. But their heroic power is double-edged, because it can also lead to less desirable qualities: excessive anger, violence, cruelty, pride, recklessness, and egotism. So there is a tension within heroism itself in that the very energy which makes the heroes outstanding is also the source of their instability and danger (both to themselves and to others). The *Iliad* and *Odyssey* are sophisticated epics, which not only celebrate the heroic world but also explore the complex nature of heroism itself.

The central action of the *Iliad* is Achilles' anger with his fellow Greeks for failing to honour him, and his subsequent withdrawal from battle. When he refuses to fight, even though the Greeks are in desperate need, his friend Patroclus takes his place, but is killed by the Trojan leader Hector. Achilles is consumed by grief and finally returns to the battlefield, driven by a desire for vengeance. However, he displays a dehumanizing rage, for he does more than kill Hector, he mutilates his corpse, dragging it behind his chariot. This is a shocking act, which violates a basic taboo protecting a dead man's body, and threatens Hector's right to burial. It takes the intervention of the gods to end Achilles' shameful conduct, for their concern leads to the meeting between Achilles and Hector's father, Priam, and to the release of Hector's corpse. And it is in this encounter with the enemy that Achilles finally regains the attitudes of pity and respect which, the *Iliad* insists, are essential qualities of the man of honour. Priam appeals to Achilles in the name of his father Peleus, and as Achilles sees the grief and suffering of his own father mirrored in the Trojan king, the two men weep together:

> So the two remembered, Priam crouched at Achilles' feet
> and weeping loud for man-slaying Hector,
> while Achilles wept for his own father, and then again
> for Patroclus; and the sound of their groaning filled the hut.
>
> (*Iliad* 24.509–12)

By showing Priam the respect due to him and to Hector, Achilles emerges from his disastrous self-obsession and grief, and recognizes the humanity of others.

The gods' concern for mortals and their constant intervention in human affairs is one of the most striking aspects of the Homeric epics. Yet Homer's gods are not merely figures of literature: they are an expression of a coherent theology. With no established church or sacred book to prescribe religious beliefs in ancient Greece, poets played a fundamental role in shaping religious ideas, and none more so than Homer, who was the foundation of all education, including what the Greeks thought about their gods. But to understand Greek religion, it is essential that we jettison inappropriate (especially Christian) conceptions of the divine as intrinsically kind and caring. For although the Greek (and Roman) gods do care for humans, they are anything but selfless, and their honour is every bit as important to them as it is to the heroes. If a god's honour is damaged, as when the Trojan prince Paris insults Hera and Athena by choosing Aphrodite as the most beautiful goddess (*Iliad* 24.25–30), they are no less relentless than the angriest of heroes in their pursuit of revenge, and their greater power means that their retribution is all the more terrifying. Thus Hera strikes a grim bargain with her husband Zeus, the chief god, offering up her three favourite Greek cities for destruction (Argos, Sparta, and Mycenae) as long as Troy is obliterated (4.50–4), and she declares her hatred of the Trojans in matter-of-fact terms (18.367): 'How could I not weave trouble for the Trojans, given my anger against them?'

The gulf between mortal and immortal is stark: the gods enjoy eternal vitality, humans face oblivion in Hades. This essential difference, the certainty of death for humans, is powerfully expressed in a simile by Glaucus, an ally of the Trojans:

> As are the generations of leaves, so also are those of men:
> the wind scatters the leaves on the ground, but the forest
> burgeons and grows others when the season of spring comes round.
> So with the generations of men, one grows and another passes away.

$$(Iliad\ 6.146–9)$$

However, it is paradoxically the very mortality of the heroes which gives them a seriousness and tragic intensity which the gods lack. Since the gods are 'sure to live forever, ageless and immortal', they face no risk of serious loss. In other words, the power and immortality of the gods mean that they cannot display courage and endurance the way humans must, and so they are diminished in comparison to them. As one ancient critic put it, 'Homer has done his best to make the men of the *Iliad* gods and the gods men' ('Longinus', *On the Sublime* 9.7).

While the *Iliad* portrays the pressures of the battlefield, the *Odyssey* explores a different form of heroism through the figure of Odysseus, 'the man of many wiles', who has to use intelligence and guile to overcome the many obstacles that keep him from returning to his home and family. The *Odyssey* is thus a variation on the tale of the wandering and returning hero which is known from many cultures around the world. In this story-pattern the hero is typically stranded far from home, and his family suffers in his absence, yet the hero battles against the odds and reclaims his wife and household. Thus the *Odyssey* begins ten years after the end of the Trojan War, but Odysseus has still not returned and his household is in disarray: a gang of over 100 disorderly and arrogant suitors is vying with one another to claim Odysseus' wife Penelope, and his young son Telemachus is unable to stop them.

The first half of the poem presents Odysseus' adventures since the fall of Troy, and we see his return to Ithaca repeatedly threatened: in the land of the Lotus-Eaters, for example, whose delicious lotus fruit makes the eater lose all memory of home, or in the cave of the monstrous Cyclops, Polyphemus, who kills and eats many of Odysseus' crew, or on the island of the witch Circe, who turns Odysseus' men into pigs and keeps the hero as her lover for a year. The second half presents Odysseus' struggle on Ithaca, disguised as a beggar, to regain his home and his heroic identity, as he and his son Telemachus slaughter the suitors, and Odysseus and Penelope are finally reunited after 20 years apart.

So whereas the *Iliad* portrays the tragic destruction of an entire society (the kingdom of Troy), the *Odyssey* is a more romantic and optimistic tale of a hero whose return to his community

24

restabilizes it. But despite its more domestic setting, the *Odyssey* is still concerned with the same concepts of honour and revenge that dominate the *Iliad*, for the shameful behaviour of the suitors cannot go unpunished. Despite repeated warnings, the suitors persist in their outrageous abuse of the hospitality of Odysseus' household and even scheme to murder Telemachus. Their complete massacre has struck some modern critics as excessive, but is fully in line with the ethics of ancient Greek society, where punishment is harsh but predictable (the suitors know well the liberties they are taking) and therefore justified.

Of course, the ultimate goal of Odysseus' mission, and the climax of the narrative, is his reunion with Penelope. Throughout the poem it is made clear that Penelope is not only stunningly beautiful (the suitors go wild whenever she appears to them in the banqueting hall), but also highly intelligent. Indeed she proves herself more than a match for the clever Odysseus himself, whom she ultimately outwits. For as he stands before her, bespattered with the blood of the suitors, she refuses to believe that this man is her husband. Knowing, however, that their marriage bed is immovable, since Odysseus had built it from the trunk of an olive tree when the house was first constructed, Penelope orders that it be moved, which prompts the angry Odysseus to tell the story of the bed's making (a secret shared by him and Penelope), thus confirming his identity for his wife. Penelope's trick shows her to be her husband's equal in cleverness and the skilled use of language, and thus proves their worthiness to be reunited as husband and wife.

Several centuries separate Homer from the author of the next complete surviving epic, Apollonius Rhodius, whose *Argonautica* was composed around 270–245 BC. In four books Apollonius narrates the Argonauts' heroic quest for the Golden Fleece, the relic of a magical ram, guarded by a monstrous, unsleeping serpent. Jason and his men sail from Iolcus in Greece to the court of king Aeetes of Colchis at the far eastern edge of the Black Sea (modern Georgia), where Jason and Medea, the king's daughter, fall in love and Medea secures the Fleece and escapes with Jason back to Greece. This was an ancient myth: Homer had used Jason's adventures as a model for those of Odysseus, and Apollonius in turn reworks Homer to create an epic with all the learning and refinement typical of the Hellenistic 'Alexandrian' style (see Chapter 1).

In reaction to what they saw as the hackneyed, bloated, and repetitive epics of Homer's inferior successors, the Alexandrian poets developed the genre in new ways, with an emphasis on the small-scale, subtle, and allusive. Reaction to played-out styles is often the driver of literary change (compare Romanticism's rejection of neoclassical 'rules', for example), and Apollonius' epic is a revolutionary and highly sophisticated renewal of the genre. The poet's erudition is proudly displayed, as he incorporates new discoveries in science, geography, and historical research into his heroic tale: Aphrodite possesses a cosmic globe that was the cutting-edge of astronomy in Apollonius' time (3.131–41); the Argonauts' return to Greece takes them along the Danube, Po, and Rhone rivers, while they must even carry their ships across the Libyan desert; and the poem is replete with stories explaining the origins of contemporary rituals, place-names, and monuments. It is easy to see why the Ptolemies of Egypt appointed Apollonius to the prestigious posts of chief librarian and royal tutor.

Whereas Homer's Odysseus is famously the man 'of many resources', the narrator of the *Argonautica* describes Jason as 'without resources' or 'at a loss', and he often seems overwhelmed by his mission. As a result Apollonius' Jason has been written off as sub-heroic and insipid, but this is to miss the point: Apollonius knows that his audience are familiar with the wider myth of Jason and Medea, in which Jason will eventually betray his wife for another woman, prompting Medea to murder her own and Jason's children in revenge, and so Jason's reliance on Medea's support gives Apollonius' account of their love affair a tragic irony. It is generally agreed that the highlight of the poem is Book 3, where the young and impressionable Medea is love-struck by the handsome stranger. Apollonius depicts her passion from the inside out, describing the psychology and physiology of desire in terms that reflect the latest Hellenistic medical theory: Medea's anguish sears through her, 'around her fine/nerves and deep below the nape of the neck/where the pain enters most agonizingly' (3.762–4). Apollonius' portrait of the love-sick and vulnerable heroine was to prove a hugely important contribution to the genre of epic, especially in its influence on Virgil's Dido.

We know nothing about Latin epic before Livius Andronicus' version of the *Odyssey* around the middle of the 3rd century BC. Although we can be confident that local Italian songs of great ancestors and heroes of old had existed for generations, nothing of them has survived and the genre of Latin epic is already thoroughly Hellenized by the time of Livius. By the same token, however, Livius' work, a literary translation of Homer, is also a thoroughly Roman creation, adapting Greek myth to express Roman values: thus, for example, the standard Homeric description of heroes as 'equal to the gods' did not fit Roman religious feelings, so Livius replaces it with 'greatest and of the first rank'. Soon afterwards Naevius wrote the first Latin epic with native Roman subject matter: his *Punic War* reflects not only his own experience as a soldier in the struggle with Carthage, but also inaugurates the Romans' greater preference (in comparison to Greeks) for historical, or at least quasi-historical, epic rather than tales set in the legendary past.

Epic was the perfect genre in which to commemorate Rome's remarkable military success and expansion in this period. Thus, the most important Latin epic before Virgil, Ennius' *Annals*, covers the whole of Roman history from Aeneas' arrival in Italy after the fall of Troy down to shortly before Ennius' own death in 169 BC, by which time Rome was the dominant power in the Mediterranean world. Ennius begins by boldly telling of a dream in which Homer's ghost appeared to him and revealed that he had been reincarnated in (conveniently) Ennius. But this aspiring Roman Homer has also read his Alexandrian Greek poets and aligns himself with their sophisticated learning, styling himself *dicti studiosus*, the Latin equivalent of 'literary scholar'. Ennius' account of Rome's rise to power made his epic the embodiment of Roman values, and Rome's militaristic elite were schooled in pithy quotations such as 'On manners and on men of old stands firm the Roman state', where the first letters of the first four words of the Latin (*moribus antiquis res stat Romana virisque*) spell out MARS, the god of war. Ennius' poem became an instant classic and was a school text for generations of Romans until it was superseded by Virgil's *Aeneid*.

Virgil's epic tells how the Trojan hero Aeneas finds his way to Italy and struggles to establish a new home there which will be the origin of Rome. It is thus a foundation narrative, like the story of the Pilgrim Fathers in the United States. The legend of Aeneas in Italy can be traced back to the 6th century BC, but as Rome's power expanded it became a basic element of Roman history and identity, and Virgil, like Naevius and Ennius before him, rewrites the myth to express the anxieties and hopes of his times (see Figure 2). As Virgil composed the poem in the 20s BC, he gave readings of his work in progress, and its quality was immediately recognized and celebrated: his fellow poet Propertius, for example, declared that 'a work greater than the *Iliad* is being brought to birth' (2.34.66). And indeed Virgil's epic soon achieved a status and authority in Roman literature and culture which rivalled that of Homer for the Greeks, so that almost every ancient writer after Virgil (whether of poetry or prose, pagan or Christian) engages at some point in creative dialogue with the *Aeneid*.

In the first half of the epic (Books 1–6) we see the Trojan fleet, bound for Italy, driven by a storm to Carthage in north Africa, where Aeneas tells Queen Dido of the fall of Troy and his people's subsequent years of wandering in search of a new home. Dido and

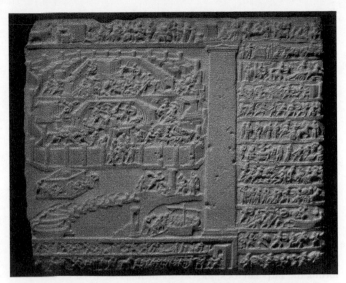

2. A miniature marble tablet from near Bovillae (some 12 miles south-east of Rome), late 1st century BC, showing the fall of Troy and Aeneas' departure 'to the west' in search of a new home. An impressive work of craftsmanship, the tablet's surviving portion (roughly 11 inches square) is inscribed with around 250 figures and depicts scenes from the *Iliad* and other Greek epics about the destruction of Troy

Aeneas fall in love, the hero forgets his mission, and Jupiter must send Mercury to remind him. But when Aeneas leaves, Dido kills herself, cursing Aeneas and his descendants. Aeneas then gains access to the underworld, where the ghost of his father Anchises reveals to him a vision of the future greatness of Rome. The second half (Books 7–12) portrays the hero's struggles in Italy itself. Aeneas is well received by Latinus, king of the Latins (one of the tribes of Italy), who accepts his embassy of peace and offers Aeneas his daughter Lavinia in marriage. But others, including Lavinia's mother, Amata, resent the Trojan immigrants and war soon breaks out. Aeneas visits Evander, whose city is located on the future site of Rome, and Evander entrusts his young son Pallas to him as a fledgling warrior in the war to come. However, Turnus, leader of the hostile Italian tribes, kills Pallas, plunging Aeneas into a frenzy of violence. When Aeneas and Turnus eventually meet in single combat, Aeneas is victorious and is on the point of sparing Turnus, who is begging for his life, when he sees the sword-belt of Pallas, which Turnus had stripped from the young man's body. In a final paroxysm of love, shame, and anger, Aeneas kills Turnus.

Whereas earlier Roman epic had catalogued the great events of Roman history in serial fashion up until the author's own day, Virgil follows the lead of Homer and creates a more complex and interesting narrative, set in the legendary past but looking forward to the history of Rome. Though Rome itself was founded long after Aeneas by Romulus and Remus, the *Aeneid* is full of foreshadowings of Roman buildings, rites, and customs, especially when Aeneas visits the future site of Rome (Book 8), where we hear of the Roman forum, the Tarpeian rock, the Capitoline hill, and so on.

And just as Homer had presented the glory of warfare but also its victims, so Virgil succeeds in creating an epic which celebrates Rome and Roman power while also confronting the traumatic aspects of its history, especially the recent civil wars. Jupiter promises the future Romans, who are created from the fusion of Italian and Trojan peoples, 'empire without end' (1.279), and Anchises explains how that empire should be run:

> But you, Roman, remember by your power to rule
> the peoples of the earth, as these will be your arts:
> to pacify and impose the rule of law,
> to spare the conquered and war down the proud. (*Aeneid* 6.851–3)

However, such a vision of orderly rule is at odds with the poem's wider depiction of Rome's origins, where future Romans (Italians and Trojans) slaughter each other, and where largely sympathetic figures like Dido, who stand in the way of Rome, are destroyed.

The *Aeneid*'s reflections on both the glories and disasters of Roman history are encapsulated in its presentation of Augustus himself. Augustus, as a member of the Julian clan, claimed descent from Aeneas' son Iulus, and several passages in the poem hail him as restoring peace to Rome, even as inaugurating a second Golden Age in Roman history—so says Anchises, in a vision of future Roman heroes revealed to Aeneas in the underworld. Augustus' victory in the civil wars did bring peace (on his terms, of course) to a war-torn Rome and there is no reason to suspect the *Aeneid*'s expressions of gratitude to him for achieving this. Yet because the poem's exploration of loss and suffering is even more striking, this has led many to discuss its politics as if the dominant question were how pro- or anti-Augustan the poem is. However, such an approach is too narrow, since the subject of the poem is much more the chaos and trauma of generations of civil war, rather than Augustus himself.

This is best seen in the final, shocking scene of the poem, where Aeneas is overcome with rage and kills the defenceless Turnus. Despite his father's advice 'to spare the conquered', Aeneas cannot show the pity which the rest of the *Aeneid*, like the *Iliad*, presents as morally admirable. From one perspective Aeneas' anger is understandable and even justifiable, since it is sparked by the urge to avenge Turnus' killing of Pallas. But Virgil has carefully framed the final combat as one of like killing like, and these images of *self*-destruction make the final scene a vivid embodiment of the carnage of Rome's civil wars. So the *Aeneid* mingles hope for the future and longing for peace—for example, as the killing of Turnus ends the war in heroic age Italy, so may Augustus' victory end the bloodletting in contemporary Rome—with an awareness that violence could easily break out again, as shown by Aeneas' final act.

All writers of Latin epic after Virgil had to figure out how to engage with his achievement. Ovid responded to the challenge by taking an even bigger theme (the whole of cosmic history, no less) and by exploiting the malleability of the epic genre as never before, creating in his *Metamorphoses* a work of such diversity that it would later be described as mock-epic or even anti-epic. In 15 books the *Metamorphoses* narrates the history of the universe from its creation down to Ovid's own day (the poem was completed just before Augustus sent Ovid into exile in AD 8), but does so in an ingenious manner, through the telling of more than 250 Greek and Roman myths of metamorphosis, from Apollo's pursuit of Daphne and her escape through transformation into a laurel tree in Book 1, down to the deification of Julius Caesar in Book 15. While Virgil had incorporated many other genres into his epic, as when the love affair of Dido and Aeneas is infused with both love poetry and tragedy, Ovid takes this process even further, creating a particularly hybrid form of epic to match his theme of change from one form into another.

Sex and humour are particularly dominant motifs, since many transformations are prompted by desire—often a god's for a woman, highlighting male/divine cruelty and carelessness—and the narrative style is crammed with verbal wit and wordplay. Ovid even has fun with the *Aeneid*, packing the fall of Troy (to which Virgil devoted an entire book) into just four words: 'Troy fell, Priam too' (*Troia simul Priamusque cadunt*, 13.404). As a history of the world in the form of Greco-Roman myth, the *Metamorphoses* is a stunning example of the Roman transformation of Greek culture, and as an encyclopedia of myth, recast in Ovid's highly visual imagination, its influence on later artists as well as writers has been enormous. Yet it is also one of the most enigmatic of ancient literary texts, since Ovid's pervasive wit makes it hard to tell how serious his jokes about Caesar and Augustus are meant to be, or how profound his questioning of human identity (what separates human from divine, or man from beast, and so forth). Modern interpretations are often very nifty, seeing ideological resistance at every turn, but one gets the impression that Ovid's ghost may be laughing up his toga sleeve at their solemnity.

Dialogue with the *Aeneid* (and with the *Metamorphoses*) is a defining feature of the major Latin epics of the 1st century AD: Lucan's *Civil War*, written under Nero; and Statius' *Thebaid*, Valerius Flaccus' *Argonautica*, and Silius Italicus' *Punica*, all written under the Flavian dynasty (the reigns of Vespasian and his sons Titus and Domitian). Though all tailor their subject matter, whether historical or mythical, to the contemporary Roman world, it is Lucan's epic which succeeds best not only in creating a distinctive style—baroque in its rhetoric, gothic in its violence and its revelling in the supernatural and the grotesque—but also in continuing the *Aeneid*'s project of exploring the legacy of Rome's civil wars. In the poem's opening lines Lucan describes his theme, the conflict between Caesar and Pompey that destroyed the republic, as 'wars...worse than civil wars, and legality conferred on crime' (1.1–2). Drawing on the violence and spectacle of the arena, the narrator speaks of 'the gladiatorial pair we always have, freedom and Caesar' (7.695–6) and shows how freedom (*libertas*) is finally annihilated. The qualified hope of the *Aeneid* that Augustus would create a better and less violent society is undone, as the imperial system that resulted is shown to have made Lucan and his contemporaries the slaves of a tyrant. Lucan's epic is often called an 'anti-*Aeneid*', but that is to neglect Virgil's own anxiety about future violence; nonetheless, the *Civil War* is an unflinching exploration of the 'madness' (*furor*) that Lucan sees as the leitmotif of Roman history since the rise of ambitious warlords in the late republic. Discovered to be part of a conspiracy to replace Nero with another (less autocratic) emperor, Lucan committed suicide in AD 65, aged only 25.

For ancient readers the genre of epic was defined by verse form (poetry written in dactylic hexameters, the distinctive metre of epic) rather than by subject matter. And so let us conclude by considering a rather different form of ancient epic—namely, didactic epic—whose ostensible aim was to instruct the reader in subjects as varied as farming, hunting, philosophy, and science. Despite the variety of topic, all didactic poetry is characterized by a teacher–pupil dynamic, which is founded on the relationship between the poet and his addressee (or 'pupil') within the poem and extends to us the reader (or 'pupil') outside it. Nobody likes to be lectured, so the internal addressee allows the poet to get his message across without seeming to browbeat his audience. This basic triangulation is handled in different ways by each poet, so that the reader is usually guided to identify with the addressee but may also see him as a model to be avoided.

We see the latter idea, whereby the reader is encouraged to do better than the internal addressee, in the earliest surviving didactic poem, the *Works and Days*, a meditation on self-improvement and honest work written by Hesiod (a near contemporary of Homer's) in the early 7th century BC, in which Hesiod lectures his wastrel brother Perses on how to sort his life out. Hesiod's persona and his brother's are carefully constructed to suit the poem's central themes of hard work and justice: Hesiod is a gruff, tell-it-like-it-is farmer—thus his hometown of Ascra in central Greece is 'bad in winter, unbearable in summer, no good at any time' (640)—while Perses is lazy and financially corrupt.

Like the biblical myth of the Fall, Hesiod's myths of Prometheus' disobedience to Zeus (which is punished by the creation of the first woman, the beguiling but deceitful Pandora) and the five ages of mankind (golden, silver, bronze, heroic, iron—with us stuck in the tough iron age) serve to explain why work is necessary and honesty best. Although Hesiod offers some practical instruction on agriculture and the days considered lucky or unlucky for various tasks (hence the 'works' and 'days' of the poem's title), this is not a technical handbook, but a sophisticated literary work which uses the tropes of a farmers' almanac—age-old proverbs (e.g. 'Give to the one who gives, but don't give to the one who doesn't') and wry humour ('Don't let a woman who flaunts her arse deceive you with her flattering chatter: she is after your barn')—in order to bolster and enliven its presentation of popular Greek wisdom and morality.

34

The earliest surviving didactic epic in Latin, Lucretius' *On the Nature of the Universe*, completed in the 50s BC, is not only a successful poem on atomic theory and its ramifications (a rare feat in itself) but also one of the greatest works of Latin literature. Poetry, Lucretius explains, makes his technical subject matter more palatable, and he speaks of coating his philosophy 'with the sweet honey of the Muses', as when a doctor puts honey on the rim of a cup to entice children to drink bitter medicine. Lucretius' mission is to convert the reader to Epicureanism, that is, the all-embracing theory of the world and our place in it advanced by Epicurus, a Greek philosopher active around 300 BC. The six-book epic is carefully structured, moving from the micro- to the macrocosmic level, from the atom and its compounds (Books 1 and 2), through the human mind, soul, and senses (Books 3 and 4), to the creation of our world and the development of civilization (Books 5 and 6). Lucretius shows that the entire universe consists of atoms (indivisible bits of matter, infinite in number) and void (empty space, infinite in extent), and goes on to elaborate such concepts as the 'swerve', a random and unpredictable movement of atoms explaining how we have free will, and the claim that there are many worlds besides our own, ideas not a million light years away from modern quantum theory.

Thankfully, however, the aim of the poem is not to help us pass a physics exam, but to achieve happiness by saving us from irrational fear, especially our fear of death and the gods, which Lucretius sees as the two most pernicious aspects of human society. Accordingly, he puts forward over 30 different arguments for the mortality of the soul, arguing (against the fear of death) that since we were not here before birth and won't be here after death, it would be foolish for us to fear what we won't be around to experience. And like Epicurus, he argues *not* that the gods do not exist, but that they do exist but do not concern themselves with human affairs, for to do so would disrupt their famously 'blessed' existence. Lucretius' indictment is not of the gods but of the corrupt religious system created in their name by humans, in which priests and their myths stop us from investigating the true nature of the universe—a debate between science and religion that continues today. But the greatest challenge to contemporary Romans lies in Lucretius' condemnation of the greed, corruption, and ambition that were about to plunge Roman society into a catastrophic civil war. The poet despises wealthy politicians and warlords like Caesar and Pompey:

> They amass a fortune through the blood of fellow citizens
> and greedily multiply their wealth, heaping death upon death.

> (3.70–1)

Lucretius' response to the corruption and violence of public life is radical: only by withdrawing from the rat-race of Rome can one escape the materialism of contemporary society and the poverty, both intellectual and ethical, of what passes as 'success' in modern life. *Plus ça change*.

Our final example of didactic poetry is Virgil's *Georgics* (from the Greek *georgica*, meaning 'things to do with farming'), which draws on both Hesiod and Lucretius. Like Hesiod's *Works and Days*, the poem purports to offer practical advice on agriculture and praises the life of the simple peasant farmer; and like Lucretius, Virgil explores humanity's place in the world, especially our relationship to the natural environment, and how we might achieve happiness within it. Virgil treats crops and weather-signs (Book 1), trees and vines (2), livestock (3), and finally the keeping of bees (4), stressing the moral values attached to *labor* ('hard work'), particularly as a means of transforming the hostile natural world for our benefit. But at the same time the metaphors of force and coercion used to describe humanity's taming of nature point to the destabilizing effects of violence in human life itself.

Written in the late 30s BC, and completed after Octavian's (the future Augustus') crucial victory at Actium in 31 BC, the *Georgics* resembles the later *Aeneid* in its focus on the chaos of the civil wars and the struggle for a balanced and more peaceful society. Virgil stresses that these conflicts represent a natural as well as a human catastrophe, as the countryside is devastated by war:

> so many wars in the world,
> so many types of crime, no proper respect for the plough,
> the fields rot in neglect with their farmers led far away,
> the curved sickles forged into steely swords. (1.505–8)

And as in the *Aeneid*, Virgil here presents Octavian as the only source of hope, as the renewer of the Italian countryside and the whole Roman world, while also acknowledging how fragile such hope is, since no reader would be unaware of Octavian's part in the bloodshed of the recent civil wars, and the stability of the 'Augustan peace' was still far away.

Epic

Chapter 3
Lyric and personal poetry

This chapter will focus on a wide range of poetry, from early Greek lyric to Roman love elegy. What unites these various forms is their basis in the world of the speaker (the 'I' of the poem), whose ideas and experiences come to the fore. For whereas genres like epic and tragedy typically focus on the mythical past, where the 'I' of the poet is foregrounded only occasionally (as in epic) or not at all (as in tragedy), much of the poetry in this chapter appears to spring from the speaker's feelings and responses in the here and now.

At first sight this kind of poetry seems highly familiar to us. The Enlightenment's emphasis on the individual as socially, politically, and artistically determinative culminated in the Romantic idea that spontaneous, genuine feeling is the basis of the best or truest poetry. Wordsworth's famous definition of poetry, in the Preface to his *Lyrical Ballads* (1802), as 'the spontaneous overflow of powerful feelings', encapsulates a conception of the art, as founded on the poet's personal emotional response to the world, which remains influential today. However, while ancient lyric or personal poetry purports to express the speaker's response to the world, and while it no doubt draws on the poet's (and audience's) personal experience of love or war (and so on), the goal of the ancient poet is not to reflect on his own experience, but to construct a *persona* which the audience will find both credible and gripping.

In other words, we need to beware the biographical fallacy when reading ancient lyric or 'personal' poetry. We saw in the last chapter, for example, how Hesiod created the personae of cantankerous farmer and wastrel brother to suit the needs of his didactic poem *Works and Days*, and in lyric or personal poetry we see the same process on a much wider scale, as the poets adopt a huge variety of personae, but all of them suited to their chosen genre (e.g. Archilochus' songs of abuse), to their performance context (aristocratic symposium, public festival, etc.), and to the goal of the narrator (be that Pindar praising victorious athletes in choral hymns, or Catullus lamenting the infidelity of his mistress).

We should also beware the idea that because much of this poetry is (or purports to be) 'personal', it is somehow less traditional or less concerned to interact with earlier literary works. Again this is a modern notion: the philosopher Immanuel Kant, for example, claimed that 'Among all the arts poetry holds the highest rank. It owes its origins almost entirely to genius and is least open to guidance by precept or examples' (*Critique of Judgement*), expressing a conception of poetry as the pure expression of the individual, not subject to literary tropes and traditions—the very opposite of ancient poets, lyric or otherwise, who are always aware of what genre they are writing in and its history.

Let us begin with ancient Greek lyric poetry. The word 'lyric' here is a catch-all term, for it embraces all early Greek poetry that is not epic or drama, and thus covers a variety of poetic forms, displaying a myriad personae. It is conventional to sub-divide these works into smaller genres—iambus, elegy, and lyric poetry proper, both solo and choral (see later)—but this should not obscure the fact that a poet is free to compose in the different forms as he or she thinks fit: thus Archilochus wrote both iambus and elegy, while Sappho composed both solo songs (for example, personal poems of love) and choral works (such as marriage hymns). So these categories are artificial, may mask continuities between the different forms, and are based on different features—'lyric' on the idea of song, elegy on metre, iambus on subject matter—but they can still be helpful in giving us an overview of the 'song culture' of early Greece.

The main performance venues for these different forms of poetry were the symposium and the public festival. The symposium was an upper-class drinking party, where elite males could listen to poets or perform themselves. A 'symposiarch', or 'leader of the drinking', was chosen, who determined how strong the wine would be (i.e. how much water would be added) and was in charge of making sure things didn't descend into drunken chaos. Women were present, but not wives, and slaves and courtesans might provide musical accompaniment or other services—the latter are (porno-)graphically depicted on surviving wine bowls and drinking cups. Civic festivals, on the other hand, were public holidays, where the whole community enjoyed not only large-scale animal sacrifice (eating meat was a treat, not an everyday occurrence), but also athletic, musical, and poetic competitions.

Turning now to the individual sub-genres of lyric, the term iambus may have been originally connected to a traditional type of jesting and ribald poetry performed at festivals of Demeter and Dionysus (deities associated with sex and fertility, among other things). But the scope of surviving iambic poetry shows that the genre developed well beyond any cultic origins to embrace a variety of themes and purposes. Mockery and abuse are prominent features, as are sexual obscenity and explicitness (the word 'motherfucker', for example, occurs only in iambus), but we also find animal fable, and moral and political exhortation. The relatively 'low' or popular linguistic register of iambus made it an ideal medium for democratic politics: thus the Athenian politician and poet Solon—active in the early 6th century BC, and later hailed as the founding hero of democracy—defends his political and economic reforms in iambic verse, claiming (among other achievements) to have liberated those Athenians who had been enslaved to wealthy masters because of debt.

The variety of iambus is clearly seen in the genre's outstanding exponent, Archilochus, who worked in the mid-7th century BC and whose reputation in antiquity was such that he was named alongside Homer as one of the greatest of poets. Famous for the energy and wit of his invective poetry, Archilochus' mockery can also have a serious edge, as when he pokes fun at the aristocratic ideal of the 'beautiful and good' man, an ideology in which beauty, nobility, and excellence all go together:

> I don't like a general who's tall or has a swaggering gait
> or preens himself on his wavy curls or has a dainty beard.
> No, let mine be a little bloke with bandy-looking legs,
> standing firm on his feet and full of guts. (fr. 114)

The iambic idea of mockery as something that gets under the surface of things to reveal the truth is here turned on the handsome, aristocratic army commander, who merely looks the part.

Archilochus also exploits his audience's knowledge of animals, especially as shaped by the folklore tradition of the animal fable, to produce allusive and compressed imagery:

> The fox knows many tricks, the hedgehog only one—but it's a big
> one. (fr. 201)

As here, Archilochus often identifies himself with the apparently weaker animal who ends up besting his enemy. The hedgehog's 'one big thing' is to curl up into a spiky ball, and the parallel with the narrator is made explicit elsewhere:

> But one big thing I know:
> to pay back with terrible harm the one who harms me. (fr. 126)

The message is clear: if you try to hurt Archilochus, not only can he protect himself, but he can do so (like the hedgehog) in a way that will cause you pain—including, it is implied, by producing abusive poetry about you.

One of the most famous series of poems by Archilochus concerned his relationship to one Lycambes and his daughters. According to ancient tradition, which read the poems autobiographically, Lycambes had betrothed his daughter Neoboule to Archilochus but later broke the agreement. Archilochus took revenge by claiming to have had sex with both Neoboule and her sister, and destroyed the reputations of both the girls (as promiscuous) and their father (as an oath-breaker), such that the whole family committed suicide out of shame. In one poem the narrator rejects his former fiancée, Neoboule, as damaged goods ('she makes many men her friends') and seduces her younger sister instead (fr. 196a). The end of the poem is simultaneously explicit and ambiguous: 'I shot my white might off, just touching golden hair.' This creates suspense and interest among the audience (tipsy men at drinking parties, or boisterous festival crowds), who are encouraged not only to speculate among themselves exactly what happened, but also to look forward to the next raunchy instalment by Archilochus in the tale of Lycambes and his daughters. Such iambic invective is not only titillating, however, for it also encodes basic moral values for an archaic Greek audience—as here concerning the keeping of promises, the importance of policing the chastity of unmarried girls, and the value of sexual restraint (for women, of course, to suit the double standards of a patriarchal society).

Unlike iambus, which is defined by its content rather than its metrical form, elegy covers all poetry written in the elegiac couplet, which was one of the most popular poetic forms throughout antiquity. Greek elegy was usually sung to the accompaniment of the *aulos*, an oboe-like instrument, two of which were played at the same time by a single musician (or aulete). We must not think of 'elegy' in the modern sense of a mournful song or poem, for although it was associated with laments and epitaphs in antiquity (the origin of our modern definition), elegy was a highly flexible form and is used for a huge variety of subjects, from mythological or historical narrative to the perennial sympotic themes of wine, women (plus boys), and song.

As with Archilochus in his iambic verse, we find elegiac poets adopting a variety of personae to suit both occasion and audience. One of the most striking is that presented in the elegies of Theognis, a poet of the late 7th century BC, who plays the role of an embittered aristocrat, a man who has lost his estates in a pro-democracy revolution and, forced into exile, now plans his revenge. Theognis addresses his mutterings to his young male lover, Cyrnus, who is urged to listen and learn. A typical complaint runs:

> Cyrnus, this city is still a city, but the common people are different:
> they used to know nothing about justice or laws,
> but wore tattered goatskins about their flanks
> and lived outside this city like deer.
> And now they are the gentry, Cyrnus, while the former nobility
> are now scum. Who can endure the sight of this? (53–8)

Theognis' poetry captures the anxiety of aristocratic communities throughout Greece in the archaic period, as their rule was threatened by the rise of democracies or by demagogues who rose to power on popular support and then set themselves up as tyrants. His defence of established privilege and detestation of the vulgar and the *nouveaux riches* made Theognis' elegies a popular choice at aristocratic symposia, where their performance helped build group and class solidarity in the face of threatening change.

The creation of solidarity is also important to the military elegies of Tyrtaeus, a Spartan poet of the mid-7th century BC, who urges his Spartan comrades to fight to the death in defence of their city and people: 'For it is a fine thing to die in the front line, a brave man fighting for his homeland…' (fr. 10.1–2). Tyrtaeus' poetry insists on the shame of defeat as much as the glory of victory and reflects the relentless militarism of Spartan society, which was unusual even by ancient standards. About 50 years before Tyrtaeus, in the late 8th century BC, Sparta had conquered the Messenians, a nearby people (and fellow Greeks), who were made 'helots' (or 'captured people'), a permanently enslaved national group whose forced labour made Sparta's militarized society both possible, since Spartan men were freed from work to become full-time soldiers, and necessary, to quell the permanent danger of slave rebellion. Tyrtaeus describes the enslaved Messenians as 'like donkeys worn out by their heavy loads' (fr. 6), and his poetry, written during the so-called Second Messenian War, following another rebellion, is geared to maintain their subjugation and to reinforce the militaristic values of Spartan society. His martial elegies inspired Spartan armies on campaign for centuries to come.

It is conventional to call the remaining poetry (i.e. that which is not iambus or elegy) 'lyric' poetry proper, and to further divide it into choral and monodic lyric, based on whether it is performed by a chorus or a solo singer. Sometimes it is unclear whether a poem was written for solo or choral performance, however, and what was originally choral could always be reperformed by a solo singer (at the symposium, for example). In any case, what characterizes this poetry is the importance of music and song—and, in the case of choral poetry, dance—since it was all sung to musical accompaniment, whether by the *aulos*, the lyre, or other stringed instruments.

Perhaps the most famous and fascinating of lyric poets is Sappho, who worked on the island of Lesbos in the late 7th century BC. The greatest female writer of antiquity, Sappho was praised by ancient fans as 'the tenth Muse'. She wrote in a variety of choral forms, including wedding songs and hymns to deities, but she was best known for her (mostly) solo poetry about love, especially on love between women. It is often claimed that Sappho's openly erotic relationship to her female circle also fulfilled an educative purpose, whereby her 'pupils' learned a wide range of activities that prepared them for later life as married wives and mothers, including music, adornment, and religious practices. On this model Sappho's group is seen as a female counterpart to the homosexual rites of passage which are well attested for young men in other parts of Greece in the archaic and classical periods.

Alternatively, her relationships could simply be erotic, without the need to claim a pedagogical purpose. (In other words, Sappho's addressees could be a succession of female lovers, not necessarily part of an institutionalized group.) In any case, what is clear is that Sappho's poetry celebrates physical intimacy and desire among women. In one poem, for example, she consoles a departing lover with memories of how 'on soft beds you would satisfy your longing' (fr. 94.21–3). The Victorian image of Sappho the (chaste) schoolmistress suppressed these unwanted lesbian elements—though, curiously enough, the gentlemen scholars concerned, many of them boarding-school educated, had no problem accepting a period of homosexual activity for young men in ancient Greece.

Many male lyric poets delight in a variety of lovers of both sexes, but none of them matches Sappho's insistence on the centrality of love to her existence:

Some say a troop of cavalry, or infantry,
or a fleet of ships is the most beautiful thing
in all the world; but I say
it is what one loves. (fr. 16.1–4)

Here the narrator's perspective is provocatively opposed to the 'male' values of martial glory, while another poem anatomizes the speaker's jealousy and despair as she watches her beloved in the company of a man (fr. 31). Heartbreakingly for us, only one poem of Sappho's has survived complete, in which she prays to Aphrodite to help her overcome the resistance of an unresponsive woman (fr. 1). Yet the very fragmentariness of Sappho's poetry serves to highlight the subtle simplicity and arresting beauty of her imagery: thus, for example, 'Love shook my heart like a wind falling upon oaks on a mountain' (fr. 47), 'Once again limb-loosening Love makes me tremble, that bittersweet, irresistible creature' (fr. 130), or (on her own daughter) 'I have a beautiful girl, her form like golden flowers, my precious Cleïs' (fr. 132.1–2).

Choral poetry was sung and danced by all sections of ancient Greek society (women, girls, men, and boys generally performed in separate choruses), and the collective voice of the chorus had an important role in articulating the values of the community by whom, and for whom, it was performed. Choral performance was a basic part of religious worship and festival entertainment and it marked many of the major events in the life of the individual, from wedding songs to funeral laments. Compared to solo lyric, choral poetry was written on a much larger scale and in a more elevated style, using elaborate metrical forms, complex syntax, ornate diction, and bold metaphors.

The largest surviving corpus of choral poetry is the collection of over 40 victory odes (or *epinikia*) by Pindar, which were composed to celebrate victories at the four major athletic festivals (the most prestigious being the Olympic games) in the first half of the 5th century BC. The winners who commissioned Pindar came from all around the Greek-speaking world, but were united in their desire to immortalize their success in poetry. The less elaborate odes may have been composed and performed at the festival soon after the event, but most were written for performance on the victor's return to his native city, and copies were kept by his family so that they could be reperformed in years to come (though not necessarily by a grand singing and dancing chorus, as at their premiere).

Pindar was much prized for the grandeur of his style, which can sound baroque and bombastic to modern taste, but which was considered by his patrons to be the perfect medium to commemorate the scale and brilliance of their achievements. As well as giving personal details such as previous victories by the patron or his family, the odes typically narrate an episode from myth (often one concerning the victor's native city) whose details are carefully shaped, like the poems' wider rhetoric of praise, in order to highlight the various factors—innate ability, hard work and training, morally guided ambition, support from the gods, and so on—which have led to the victor's success. Again, we may baulk at the odes' emphasis on inborn excellence and the victor's superiority to the common man, but Pindar's conservative outlook reflects and bolsters the aristocratic worldview of his wealthy and powerful patrons. At the moment of divinely aided victory, Pindar insists, human ephemerality is transcended:

> Creatures of a day. What is a man? What is he not? Shadow's dream
> is man. But when the radiance of Zeus comes,
> there is a bright light upon men, and life is sweet. (*Pythian* 8.95–7)

And yet, as human potential is realized, it is also acknowledged that success can excite envy, whether from fellow humans or the gods, and so the odes' dour (and to us surprising) insistence on human mortality and limitations also serves to protect the victor from the dangers of success.

According to the Roman philosopher and dramatist Seneca, 'Cicero said that even if his lifespan were doubled, he wouldn't have the time to read the lyric poets' (*Moral Epistles* 49.5). Fortunately, many other Romans had a greater appreciation for lyric poetry, and Latin literature has a range of lyric and personal poetry to rival that of the Greeks. Perhaps the most impressive is Catullus, who wrote during the late republic (60s to mid-50s BC), and whose oeuvre, despite its small size (116 poems), presents a huge range of poetic forms and styles, from mini-epics and religious hymns to literary parody and socio-political satire. But it is Catullus' poetry concerning his affair with the married woman whom he calls Lesbia which has always been the most popular part of his work. These 25 (mostly short) poems present various snapshots of their relationship, but not in chronological order, so it is up to the reader to piece together the story of their affair, from Catullus' initial infatuation and bliss through to disillusionment and hate, as he realizes Lesbia has been sleeping with other men besides him.

The willingness of many readers to believe in this affair, and to search for the real woman behind the literary pseudonym 'Lesbia' (an allusion to Sappho, who came from Lesbos), is a tribute to the artful spontaneity and seeming sincerity of Catullus' poetry, as when the battle between Catullus' knowledge of what Lesbia is really like and his overpowering desire for her is dramatized in just two short lines:

> *Odi et amo. quare id faciam, fortasse requiris.*
> *nescio sed fieri sentio et excrucior.*
> I hate and I love. Why do that, you may ask.
> I don't know—but I feel it and it's torture. (Poem 85)

However, the problem with such a biographical approach is that it not only neglects the literary background to the relationship, whereby what happens in it is a reworking of earlier literature (especially erotic poetry), but also risks obscuring the sexual stereotypes and ideology underlying Catullus' account, which license the male poet/narrator to engage in adultery while attacking his female partner's promiscuity. In other words, Catullus is, like the Greek lyric poets before him, creating a persona whose expressions of personal feeling and strong emotion are both recognizable and enthralling. In the Lesbia poems, Catullus' persona is that of a devoted but betrayed lover, a man who is always the victim and who places all the moral faults on the other side. Thus, for example, he describes their relationship as 'this eternal pact of sacred friendship' (*aeternum hoc sanctae foedus amicitiae*, 109.6), disguising his complicity in adultery and playing up his role as the victim of Lesbia's betrayal.

Catullus clearly intended such poetry to be shocking in its Roman context, not only in its celebration of an adulterous affair, but also in its championing of a lifestyle which, by rejecting a conventional career for an existence dominated by love and pleasure, was simultaneously unmanly and un-Roman. In loving Lesbia as he does, Catullus is defying all those stuffy old-fashioned Romans who just don't get it:

> Let us live, my Lesbia, and let us love,
> and as for the mutterings of over-strict old men
> let us value them all at a single farthing! (5.1–3)

And by entertaining his audience with an outrageous persona that breaks every rule of conventional Roman morality, Catullus paved the way for Roman love elegy, a genre of erotic poetry created by the next generation of Roman writers.

Cornelius Gallus' beloved Lycoris, Propertius' Cynthia, Tibullus' Delia and Nemesis, and Ovid's Corinna were all influenced by the patterns of obsession, jealousy, and romantic idealism developed by Catullus in his poetry about Lesbia. But each of these poets also gives his own spin to the persona of the elegiac lover and explores in his own way the possibilities of the genre. Tibullus, for example, who wrote in the 20s BC, sets his imaginary world of love in the countryside rather than the urban world of Catullus, Propertius, and Ovid. The rural setting offers a romantic and idyllic escape from the pressures of Rome, where Tibullus and his readers can enjoy the potent Roman fantasy of the simple country life. Propertius' four books show him increasingly extending the genre to include diverse themes, including Roman politics and history, thus returning elegy to its Greek roots, where it is a highly flexible form. His beloved Cynthia dominates the first two books and he bids her (and his career as a love poet) farewell at the end of Book 3, but she returns with a vengeance in Book 4—even from beyond the grave, her ghost appearing to Propertius in a dream to attack him for his infidelity. Ovid's elegiac works are sometimes labelled 'parody', since he knowingly (and ostentatiously) plays with the conventions of love elegy—the locked-out lover, the slave go-between, the rich rival, and so on—but we have to be careful that terms like 'parody' or 'deconstruction' applied to Ovid do not obscure how artificial and constructed the lover's persona is in Catullus, Tibullus, and Propertius as well.

Thus their female lovers not only have literary pseudonyms, but also serve as symbols of the tradition of love poetry itself and the poet's contribution to it. Like Catullus, the other poets are let down by their unfaithful girlfriends, who are not only beautiful, passionate, and temperamental, but also well-read—another hint at their literary role. The elegiac poets take many of the conventions of love poetry—for example, the idea that love is like war, full of battles and suffering, or a form of slavery to one's mistress—and adapt them so as to be as shocking and titillating as possible for their Roman audience. Thus Propertius proclaims love more important than loyalty to one's family or military service to the state, while Tibullus rejects the greed and power politics that lead to war: 'Love is a god of peace, we lovers honour peace', says Propertius (3.5.1), foreshadowing the 'make love, not war' idealism of later rebels. And while Catullus' obsession with the capricious and unfaithful Lesbia threatens to invert the power dynamic of established gender roles, the elegiac poets go further and positively revel in the self-abasement of their 'slavery' to love—a shocking image in a slave-owning society like Rome, where the slave is little more than a living tool of its master or mistress. Their loss of autonomy verges at times on the sado-masochistic:

> Here I see slavery to a mistress prepared for me:
> O freedom of my fathers, farewell.

I'm given to harsh slavery, I'm held in chains,
and Love, to my sorrow, never slackens my bonds,
but burns me, regardless of my guilt or innocence.
I'm burning now, aargh, cruel girl, remove the flame!
(Tibullus, *Elegies* 2.4.1–6)

The Roman (male) reader could thus enjoy the frisson of the loss of power and self-control which was a crucial part of his identity. Later Romans were proud of the Latin love elegists—'in elegy too we rival the Greeks', declared Quintilian (*Education of the Orator* 10.1.93)—and it is fair to say that these poets succeeded in creating a genre which is, like satire (see Chapter 8), distinctively Roman.

If 'making it Roman' is a crucial measure of a Latin author's success in his engagement with his Greek predecessors, then Horace's achievement in the *Epodes* and *Odes* of reinventing Greek iambic and lyric poetry for Roman readers must rank alongside Virgil's transformation of epic in the same turbulent period. The *Epodes*, written in the 30s BC, adapt the broad thematic focus of Greek iambic poetry—which, as we saw, included not only invective but a wide range of socio-political commentary—for a Rome in the grip of civil war. In *Epodes* 7 and 16, for example, probably written in the early 30s BC, Horace urges his fellow Romans to abandon their self-destructive madness, but the poet sensibly hedges his bets and does not take sides in the struggle. By contrast, in *Epodes* 1 and 9, written after the decisive battle of Actium in 31 BC, Horace celebrates the role played in it by his friend and patron, Maecenas, and buys into the emergent Augustan regime's propaganda that the war was against a decadent foreign enemy, Cleopatra, and her influence upon weak men such as Mark Antony, rather than a civil war between competing Roman dynasts.

Horace's greatest lyric achievement, however, are his four books of *Odes*, which take on the complex traditions of Greek lyric (ranging from archaic to Hellenistic styles) and recreate their musical and thematic variety for the learned literary world of Augustan Rome. With great ambition Horace states in the first poem of the collection that his aim is to be added to the Alexandrian canon of the Nine Lyric Poets:

> But if you rank me among the lyric poets,
> I shall strike the stars with my head held aloft. (*Odes* 1.1.35–6)

And in the final poem of Book 3 (Books 1–3 being published together in 23 BC) he proudly restates his success as the first Latin lyric poet, that is, as the first to have written Latin poetry in the challenging metrical forms of Greek lyric:

> Poor-born but capable,
> I was the first to recreate Aeolian song
> in Italian rhythms. (3.30.12–14)

Thus the first nine poems of Book 1 are all written in a different metre, showcasing Horace's unprecedented skill in shaping the Latin language to fit complex, non-native traditions. Moreover, Horace's insistence on the importance of music and performance also underlines his new status as a major public poet. For Horace's *Odes*, unlike his archaic Greek models, were not tied to a particular place of performance, but were written primarily to be read, and yet his repeated allusions to music, song, the poet's lyre, his audience, and so on, combine to produce the illusion of performance, creating a sense of spontaneity and shared experience (as at a symposium or civic festival) and emphasizing Horace's elevated status as a poet who, like his Greek predecessors, has the right to speak out about the life of his community.

The *Odes* reflect upon all aspects of contemporary Roman society, from religious hymns to poems about friendship, love, and politics. And, as in Greek lyric, Horace's persona changes to suit his theme, from the grand priest-poet of the religious and political odes to the avuncular and at times whimsical philosopher of the drinking party, always ready with sage advice, whether erotic or metaphysical:

> Be wise, strain the wine, and since time is brief, reduce far-reaching hope. While we're speaking, envious life will have fled: seize the day (*carpe diem*) and trust as little as possible to the time to come. (1.11.6–8)

Horace draws on all the great figures of the Greek lyric tradition, from poets as diverse as Sappho and Pindar, but it is with Alcaeus (a contemporary of Sappho's on Lesbos: see Figure 3) that Horace most frequently identifies, since he was famed as a poet of politics and war as much as friendship, love, and wine, and so best embodies the huge range of Horatian lyric.

The political revolution reflected in the *Epodes* remains central to the *Odes*, as Horace combines pity for those who died fighting for the Republican cause with numerous expressions of gratitude to Augustus for ending the civil wars and attempting to reverse the decline of Roman morality. Indeed, the idea of moving on from the civil wars, and not repeating them, is a leitmotif of all four books. And, as in Virgil's *Aeneid*, we see a combination of hope and anxiety: hope that Augustus' 'back to basics' moral and religious reforms will succeed, but fear of falling back into civil strife. Thus Horace repeatedly emphasizes the degeneration of Roman society:

> The age of our parents, worse than our grandparents, produced us, more wicked, set in due course to bring forth an even more sinful lineage. (3.6.46–8)

Ruin seems inevitable—unless, it is implied, one takes the advice given in the *Odes*. In other words, Horace (like Virgil) is not

3. An Athenian red-figure painting on a wine-cooler, *c*.480–470 BC, showing Alcaeus and Sappho, the two famous lyric poets of Lesbos, performing for one another

simply praising Augustus and his regime but trying to guide it too. Thus the *Odes*, in their astonishing poetic skill and thematic ambition, are among the most impressive creations of Latin literature, and have proved worthy of Horace's boast (at the conclusion of Books 1–3):

> I have raised a monument, more lasting than bronze,
> loftier than the pyramids' royal peaks,
> which no devouring rain or raging northerly gale
> has power to destroy, nor the uncountable
> succession of years and the flight of time. (3.30.1–5)

Chapter 4
Drama

In this chapter we shall consider two of the most popular genres of ancient literature, tragedy and comedy, and try to account for their success as forms of mass entertainment. We shall see how each of the surviving major playwrights, Greek and Roman, engages with the values of his audience, and encourages them to relate the world on stage to their own experience. So let's begin with tragedy, one of the most influential literary forms to emerge from ancient Greece, whose development is closely tied to the popular culture of Athens in the 5th century BC. The origins of tragedy are murky, but rife with scholarly speculation: fortunately, however, the issue of origins is a minor one since even if clear they would tell us nothing about the surviving plays themselves. The most we can say is that, as a form of drama which combines choral song and dance with dialogue between actors and chorus, tragedy (like comedy) is likely to have developed from choral performance. But by the time of the earliest surviving play, Aeschylus' *Persians*, produced in 472 BC, tragedy is already a developed dramatic genre and, as a form of competition poetry, where poets are continually innovating and experimenting in the hope of winning first prize, it has grown far beyond its religious or ritual origins (if such there were).

You'll notice I spoke above of 'mass entertainment' and 'popular culture', and that's because tragedy and comedy were not the rarefied preserve of a small socio-economic elite (like much theatre in modern Western society), but were performed at popular civic festivals in front of large audiences, as many as 6,000 spectators in 5th-century Athens, drawn from all sections of society. (The theatre was expanded in the late 4th century BC to hold as many as 17,000.) It is possible that women, children, and slaves were present, for example, though not in large numbers—they did not qualify for the state subsidy on tickets, so were dependent on their own wealth and the willingness of their family—and not in the posh seats up front, which were reserved for male Athenian citizens and for VIPs such as visiting dignitaries from other Greek city-states. The major venue for drama in Athens was the annual civic festival known as the City (or Great) Dionysia, which lasted five days and saw three tragedians compete against each other, each presenting four plays (usually three tragedies and a satyr play—the latter a humorous burlesque of tragic myth, featuring a chorus of rowdy satyrs, half-men, half-beast), and five comic playwrights, each with one comedy.

This was a huge state-sponsored festival—though wealthy private citizens also contributed, by paying for the training and costuming of the choruses—and the masterpieces that emerged from it are an argument for subsidizing the arts if ever there was one. The ancient dramatic texts that have survived are scripts for performance, but we have lost the music and choreography and the whole visual spectacle, which have to be re-imagined as we read. Female roles were played by adult men (rather than by boys, as in Shakespeare) and both this and the playing of multiple roles were helped by the use of masks, wigs, and costumes. As large open-air theatre, acting styles and gestures will have been bold and expressive, but no less effective or moving. The presence of a large chorus within the action itself—15 members in tragedy, 24 in comedy—creates a kind of internal audience, a watching community who are also able to interact with the central figures of the drama, and whose thoughts and reactions are no less integral to the play's meaning. Not surprisingly, this all-singing-and-dancing chorus is, along with the gods, one of the hardest things to do well in modern productions of Greek drama.

A fundamental point to bear in mind is that Greek tragedy is much more varied than modern (post-classical or neo-classical) ideas of 'the tragic' would lead one to believe. Founded on a misreading of Aristotle's *Poetics*, neo-classical scholars and dramatists invented certain 'rules' of tragedy, but these are largely useless since they bear no relation to the surviving ancient plays. Equally misleading is the attempt, especially popular since the German Romantics of the 18th century, but pre-dating them, to deduce an essentially tragic worldview (in short—no happy endings), which is then retrojected onto the ancient genre, so that those plays which don't quite come up to scratch are then re-categorized as 'romantic tragedy', 'escape tragedy', 'tragicomedy', or even 'melodrama'. But although the search for the 'truly tragic' risks taking too narrow a view of the genre, it is responding to something that all the surviving plays have in common, namely human suffering, which is present even in the so-called 'happy ending' tragedies. We have a partial analogue in Shakespeare's tragedies, which include humorous elements (though fewer happy endings), and which go against neo-classical rules and are all the more profound and moving for doing so.

So in Greek tragedy there is always suffering and the stakes are always high. The heroes who suffer exist in myth (as well as religious cult), and myth is the raw material of tragedy, already shaped by generations of epic and lyric poets, and now transformed for a new audience in a new genre. The advantages of myth are many: the audience, for example, has a shared basis for understanding—but just in case they don't know the story, the important details are always made clear at the start!—and poets can display their imagination and inventiveness in handling more or less well known material. The audience's familiarity with any given story—the myth of Oedipus, say, who unwittingly kills his father and sleeps with his mother, producing four children—does not remove suspense, but actually generates it, as they wonder how this particular poet will handle the horrific outcome they know is coming. The use of myth also allows there to be a certain (and variable) distance between the here and now of the audience and the legendary world of the play, so that distressing subject matter can be explored (war, murder, grief, incest, rape, jealousy, revenge...), and intense emotions aroused, in an imaginary space that is not so close as to become traumatic.

One of the most basic moral patterns underlying Greek tragedy is that of 'learning through suffering'. Such a concept of 'didactic' drama, of plays that make us better citizens, sounds terribly preachy to our (post-)modern selves, but it was a basic assumption of ancient thought that art in all its forms should make us better by teaching us true and useful things. Tragedy's teaching was notoriously rejected by Plato, whose ideal state would censor poetry to ensure its compliance with his moral and religious system. Plato viewed tragedy, with its vivid depiction of disaster-prone and lamenting heroes, as morally and psychologically degrading, but his particular hatred of the genre (he speaks contemptuously of 'theatocracy') is also linked to his contempt for democracy itself, as he recognizes in tragedy a major genre of popular art with broad appeal.

By contrast, Aristotle, Plato's most brilliant pupil, rejected his master's reactionary politics and aesthetics, and by insisting that human beings learn through *mimesis* (imitation, or fiction), reaffirmed tragedy's value as an art form capable of imparting important knowledge. Aristotle also observed what we might call the 'tragic paradox', that is, the way we get pleasure from viewing the suffering of others on stage: *mimesis* gives us the necessary distance to make such contemplation both pleasurable and beneficial. This issue, which has preoccupied theorists of tragedy ever since, is memorably posed by tragedy itself, when in Euripides' *Bacchae* the disguised god Dionysus asks Pentheus, as he tempts him to his doom, 'would you really like to see what gives you pain?' (815).

But the pleasure of tragedy also has an important moral and metaphysical dimension. For tragedy asks how we are to account for human suffering and gives an answer that is bracing, but not pessimistic. Crucially, tragedy is interested in disasters that spring from human choices and actions: suffering in tragedy is never merely random, as it often is in real life, but is set within a wider moral and religious framework that gives shape and meaning to human catastrophe. So it is a highly consoling genre as well as a horrific one, as we realize the universe is cruel, but not meaningless, and see the cosmic order behind the chaos, agony, and grief on stage. We might recall the *bon mot* of Samuel Johnson: 'The only end of writing is to enable the readers better to enjoy life, or better to endure it.' We emerge from viewing tragedy with our sympathies enlarged, and reminded that others have suffered worse.

In its depiction of a dysfunctional heroic world, tragedy explores the full gamut of issues from the existential (why do we suffer?) to the topical (the benefits and risks of Athenian democracy and empire). Central and recurring themes include *hybris* in all its juicy forms (i.e. thinking and acting beyond human norms); the scope and limits of human knowledge and understanding, especially in contrast to that of the gods; the causes and consequences of war, continuing the Homeric view of war as something that is both cruel and glorious; the qualities that make a good leader or a successful constitution, with a pronounced democratic bias against monarchs, tyrants, and oligarchs; the status and roles of men and women and how to manage human sexuality; ethnicity and nationalism, in the relationship between Greeks and barbarians, and between Athenians and other Greeks; and perhaps most frequently of all, the desire for revenge and its often self-destructive consequences. Let's look at two of these issues (knowledge and gender) in more detail.

Ever since Aristotle lauded Sophocles' *Oedipus Tyrannus* for its superb plot-construction and overwhelming emotional impact, the play has come to have the status of the archetypal tragedy. One ancient critic, for example, sums up Sophocles' fellow tragedian Ion by saying, 'Indeed, no one in his right mind would reckon all Ion's works put together as the equivalent of the one play, *Oedipus*' ('Longinus', *On the Sublime* 33.5). And in modern times the play was famously interpreted by Sigmund Freud as the story of a universal male fantasy—though, it has to be said, since Oedipus was in fact ignorant of his father and mother's true identity, he himself could not have had the so-called 'Oedipus complex'. Yet the play's power to shock and disturb remains undimmed, as we see Oedipus gradually discover that he has broken two of the most fundamental taboos of human society (patricide and incest), and that the things which mark his success in life—his roles as king, husband, and father—are in fact grotesque illusions that will destroy him. Oedipus' ruin is so terrifying not only because of the nature of his discovery, but also because the play forces us to recognize that we too could easily act in ignorance and commit great wrongs unintentionally. Oedipus is punished for acts he did not intend, and so the play enacts the harsh but inescapable ethical truth that, to quote an eminent modern philosopher, 'in the story of one's life there is an authority exercised by what one has done, and not merely by what one has intentionally done' (Bernard Williams, *Shame and Necessity*).

All three tragedians explore the mutually defining gender roles of their time, not only asking what is to be a good man (as husband, father, son, citizen, soldier, etc.), but also insisting on the respect due to women, especially as wives and mothers—that is, still very much within the boundaries of a fundamentally patriarchal society. No play depicts the disastrous consequences of a man's mistreatment of his wife and family more powerfully than Euripides' *Medea*, in which Jason abandons Medea and their two sons for a more advantageous match with a Greek princess, leading Medea to punish Jason's disloyalty by murdering their own children. In her opening speech, Medea outlines the injustices of women's lot: she condemns the fact that husbands are masters of their wives' bodies, points to the sexual

61

double standard that permits men, but not women, to pursue extra-marital affairs, and ends with the ringing declaration: 'I would rather stand three times with a shield in war than give birth once!' (*Medea* 230–51). One can see why Medea's speech was read aloud at suffragette rallies in the early 20th century, even if the play as a whole, in its original cultural context, is far from being a feminist work or an argument for equality in the modern sense. Nonetheless, it does dramatize the disaster that ensues when a woman's status and authority are disrespected, and excoriates Jason for his failure as a husband and father. As often in Greek tragedy, the man errs first, and reaps the consequences of violating the woman's rights. The (probably) mixed-sex audience see a dramatic world in which social breakdown is two-sided, and are led to appreciate the importance, for both sexes, of respecting the rights of the other. Thus women's perspective is clearly seen in Greek tragedy, perhaps more strongly than anywhere else in classical literature, despite the fact that the authors of the plays were men.

As with tragedy, the early stages of comedy as a literary genre are obscure. It may have developed from popular entertainments involving obscenity and invective (akin to iambic poetry, discussed in Chapter 3) around the fringes of festivals, but by the time of our earliest surviving play, Aristophanes' *Acharnians*, produced in 425 BC, it is a fully developed dramatic genre, formed (like tragedy) from a mixture of speech, song, and dance. Hellenistic scholars tried to impose order on the development of the genre by dividing it into three phases: Old, Middle, and New Comedy. Unfortunately, we can't say much at all about Middle Comedy, since there is no extant example, but the broad differences between Old Comedy (political, obscene, fantastic...) and New Comedy (domestic, restrained, realistic...) are clear, and we can see a transition between them in the last two surviving plays of Aristophanes, *Women at the Assembly* and *Wealth*, written in the early 4th century BC, which contain less obscenity, personal ridicule, and political satire than before—and also a diminishing role for the chorus, which has disappeared entirely as a character in the drama by the time of New Comedy in the late 4th century.

As tragedy has its Big Three (Aeschylus, Sophocles, Euripides), so too Old Comedy: Cratinus, Eupolis, and Aristophanes. Although only complete plays by Aristophanes survive, 11 in total (a quarter of his output), we have enough fragments of the others' works to see that they had much in common in subject matter and style. Old Comedy differed from its dramatic sibling, tragedy, in numerous ways—for example, grotesque rather than dignified masks (see Figure 4); costumes that were humorously padded at the belly and bum, complete with a dangling leather phallus (for all male roles); colloquial and obscene language; explicit metatheatre, such as references to stage machinery; asides to the audience (still a popular feature of comic plays)—but for all these differences comedy was, like tragedy, a genre that reflected on contemporary Athenian society, albeit mostly in the form of criticism and ridicule.

4. Roman wall mosaic with tragic and comic masks from Hadrian's Villa at Tibur (mod. Tivoli), begun c.AD 118 and the largest Roman villa ever built

Comedy was usually set in the here and now of the audience (rather than the distant world of myth), but its plots are full of fantasy, such as journeys to Cloudcuckooland (the newly established avian city in *Birds*) or to the Underworld (as in *Frogs*). These plays are named after their choruses of birds and frogs (so too Aristophanes' *Wasps*), and the frequent use of animals in Old Comedy as models or foils for human behaviour is another feature it has in common with iambic poetry. The comic 'hero' is not some grand figure of heroic myth (an Achilles or an Odysseus), but an ordinary Athenian, who is unhappy with some aspect of society and so hatches an ingenious plan to realize his or her dream (*Frogs* is a partial exception, in that the 'hero' is the god Dionysus, who goes down to the Underworld to fetch a tragic poet to save the city, but the god is treated irreverently throughout): thus, in *Acharnians*, for example, Dicaeopolis arranges a private peace-treaty with Athens' arch-enemy Sparta; in *Birds* two Athenians, fed up with Athens and its endless law-suits, persuade the birds to set up a new city in the sky, which is a huge success; in *Lysistrata* the eponymous Athenian heroine persuades women from several warring city-states to join her sex strike, and the desperate men are forced to make peace.

Laughter and comedy can be serious, of course, and what makes an audience laugh is revealing of their concerns and anxieties. Not surprisingly for a democratic society at war—most of Aristophanes' theatrical career was during the Peloponnesian War (431–404 BC)—there is much satire directed at the politicians and generals in charge, but democracy itself is never questioned, and the natural desire for peace does not mean peace at any price. The comedies also play with sexual stereotypes, as when the intelligent and high-minded Lysistrata is contrasted with the sex-lies-and-booze-obsessed women she has to win over to her plan. Again, as with tragedy, these comic texts are not documents of emancipation, and the plays end with the women returning to their 'natural' sphere, the home; nonetheless, they pack a punch in showing how stupid and incompetent the current male leadership can be.

Trying to describe humour risks absurdity in itself. But we can at least point to some of the typical sources and techniques used by Aristophanes to generate his gags. The first thing to stress is the sheer variety of comedy on offer—whether you like shit jokes (i.e. jokes about shitting, not...), fart jokes, slapstick pranks, and double entendres, or whether your taste runs more to sophisticated literary parody and political satire, there is something for everyone in Aristophanes, and comedy mirrors tragedy in its broad popular appeal—as one would expect, since they're on at the same festivals and both want to win first prize in their respective competition. The evergreen comic trope 'Isn't life crap nowadays? It was better when I were a lad...' is frequently deployed, as cultural change in all its forms—new styles of music, poetry, science, philosophy, and so on—is targeted, and the generation gap, usually represented by a mutually uncomprehending father and son, is a regular source of laughs.

As Aristophanes dominates our view of Old Comedy, so our understanding of New Comedy is shaped by the surviving works of Menander, an Athenian playwright whose career spanned the late 4th and early 3rd centuries BC. Although he wrote over 100 plays, Menander didn't make it into the medieval manuscript tradition, and until recently his work was known only from quotations by other ancient authors and from his influence on the Roman comic playwrights Plautus and Terence (to whom we'll return). But from the 1890s onwards (which counts as 'recently' if you're a classicist...) there has been a constant stream of newly published papyri which have transformed our view of Menander's achievement, and we now have one play, *The Old Git* (*Dyskolos*), virtually complete and significant chunks of many more. As noted above, New Comedy differs from Old in being more naturalistic in style, and it can feel rather tame in comparison: there is no invective or political satire, for example, and the exuberant leather phalluses have gone. One ancient critic summed up Menander's skilful realism by asking, 'Mendander, life: which imitated which?' So while we may miss the obscenity and surrealism of

Aristophanes, Menander's comedies have a gentler, more ironic humour and are no less revealing of ancient Greek society.

Several factors motivated New Comedy's turn away from Athenian politics to its domestic scene. Most importantly, Athens was now under Macedonian rule following the conquests of Philip and Alexander the Great, so there was no democracy, no freedom of speech, and to comment directly on politics could be risky. But to put it more positively, an art form that focuses on the typical tensions and problems of everyday life—especially family and romantic relationships—is sure to find a receptive audience, since we all live as part of families and (to quote a million cheesy songs) we all just want to be loved. Plus, many people no doubt found politics rather dull, as they do today: Jane Austen's novels, for example, tell us more about love and family life than about Luddites or local government reform in her time, but she's still the most widely read English classic. So New Comedy's turn towards love and family issues not only made it the precursor of modern domestic and romantic comedy in all their forms, but also give it a universal resonance that still appeals today.

In Menander's time (as still in Jane Austen's), love between a young man and woman was not just their affair, but something that involved the whole family, especially the fathers in the two families about to be connected. Thus the plays focus on the tensions and obstacles involved, with theatrical focus on distressing situations and last-minute revelations such as kidnapped daughters, suspected infidelity or illegitimate children, and foundling babies. Strikingly, these dramas are also full of rape, the last thing we might expect to find in a comedy: but since it threatens the life of the woman, the honour of the woman and her family, and the legitimacy of the potential child and its inheritance, rape's occurrence as a plot device in ancient domestic drama is understandable, and its use can be critical, as when Charisios in Menander's *Men Arbitrating* shockingly blames his wife, Pamphile, for being the victim of rape but is not bothered he himself has committed the same offence in the past—it being a comedy, a 'happy ending' is in order, and so Charisios is revealed to be the true father of the child, having had sex with Pamphile at a festival before their marriage, and is finally brought to regret his own double standard and his lack of compassion towards his wife. Here, as often in Menander, the final resolution of the plot's complications underlines the importance of tolerance and sympathy in human relationships.

Compared to Greek theatre, Roman drama presents an even wider range of genres, both serious and humorous: tragedy; Roman historical drama; comedy in two different forms, one based on Greek New Comedy, the other on native Italian traditions; farce, which featured stock characters (clown, braggart, glutton, hunchback, schemer, etc.) performing sketches full of silliness and obscenity, and parodies of tragedy and myth; and two genres adapted from the Greek, which became very popular under the empire: pantomime, a form more like our ballet than our 'He's behind you!' entertainment of the same name, in which a solo masked male dancer performed (usually tragic) scenes from myth to the accompaniment of musicians and chorus (*pantomimus* meaning 'he who can imitate everything'); and finally mime, which again is a very different form from ours, since in Roman mime the actors and (shockingly) actresses, without masks, performed spoken sketches, whether lewd or topical or parodying serious literary forms such as love elegy—stock elements included the 'husband, wife, her lover, and maid' scenario, the Holy Grail of modern farce.

Alas, as with Greek theatre, very little of this work survives, and our view of Roman drama is largely fragmentary and lopsided, for we have no complete Roman comedies after Plautus and Terence around 205–160 BC and no complete tragedies before Seneca in the 40s–60s AD. The comedies of Plautus and Terence are fascinating works, not only because they are the oldest complete examples of Latin literature that we have, but also because we can see in some detail for the first time the Roman transformation of a Greek genre. (As we saw in Chapter 2, only fragments of early Roman epic survive.) For although based on Greek originals, these are highly creative adaptations, and while Plautus and Terence may be reusing settings, plots, and characters from New Comedy, they are rewriting, not simply translating, and giving them their own spin in order to appeal to new, Italo-Roman audiences: Plautus proudly jokes in the prologue to *The One about the Asses*, 'Demophilus [an otherwise unknown Greek dramatist] wrote this play, Maccus [Plautus] turned it barbarian [i.e. made it Roman].' In any case, many in the audience would not know the Greek originals, so the Roman comedies had to stand or fall on their own merits. At the festivals where they were performed, plays also had to compete for the audience's attention with other popular attractions such as acrobats, tightrope walkers, boxers, wrestlers, and gladiators. We know from prologues to the plays that the audiences themselves comprised people from all social classes and age groups, women as well as men, and that they could be rowdy to the point of stopping the performance if not sufficiently entertained.

Plautus wrote around 130 comedies, of which 20 survive. What strikes one first is how different they are from the naturalistic style of Menander and Terence. With his loosely constructed plots, colourful language, puns, extensive use of sung lyrics, and frequent play with theatrical convention, Plautus is reminiscent of Greek Old Comedy, and as in Aristophanes the humour ranges from broad slapstick and physical comedy to literary parody. The figure of the 'clever slave', already found in Aristophanes, is developed much further by Plautus, who uses it in most plays. Typically the young master is at a loss as to how to get his girl, but his resourceful slave bamboozles all who stand in their way—rival lovers, slave-dealers, pimps, stern old fathers—and all's well that ends well. The Roman audience can enjoy the frisson of this topsy-turvy world, where slaves outwit their citizen superiors, but the fantasy always ends with 'normality', including the power dynamics of slavery, restored. Social and moral order always return, and bad or less sympathetic characters are foiled.

Unusually for an ancient writer, all of Terence's works, six comedies in all, have survived. A major factor here was the use of Terence's plays as school texts in antiquity and beyond, since his natural and elegant Latin and his measured moralizing were considered just the right stuff for the young—by contrast, Plautus' language is more difficult and his comedy far more risqué, akin to farce and mime. (Terence's exemplary Latin is all the more striking if, as ancient sources report, he originally came to Rome as a slave from Carthage in North Africa.) Four of Terence's six plays are based on Menander, and he was notoriously dismissed as 'half a Menander' by Julius Caesar, rather unfairly, since he not only adapts his Greek originals to appeal to Roman tastes and interests, but also skilfully combines material from more than one Greek original for a single play. Though less sexual, boisterous, and musical than Plautus' dramas, Terence's have their own comic appeal, and he polemically presents their more refined style as an advantage, flattering his audience by implying that such a learned group will naturally prefer his plays to the vulgar slapstick produced by his rivals.

Like Greek New Comedy, Roman comedy largely refrains from direct commentary on contemporary politics (let alone attacks on specific politicians, as in Old Comedy), but it nevertheless reflects and engages with basic issues affecting Roman society. As we saw in Chapter 1, the late 3rd and early 2nd century BC was a crucial and remarkable period of Roman history, as Rome's victories made it a Mediterranean superpower, and the changes (good and bad) wrought by war and empire are explored in the plays. In *The Captives* by Plautus, for example, the central characters are Greek prisoners of war who ultimately regain their freedom, as did 1,200 Romans in 194 BC, when the Roman general Flaminius rescued them from slavery in Greece, and as thousands of Roman soldiers did not after the battle of Cannae in 216 BC, when the Roman senate refused to pay Hannibal a ransom for them. Roman expansion also shaped the development of their own ethnic and cultural identity, and in plays like Plautus' *The Little Carthaginian* we see, for example, the stereotype of the duplicitous Carthaginian, as opposed to the honest, straight-talking Roman, being used for comic effect. But, as with Menander, it is Roman comedy's focus not only on the perennial problems of everyday life—especially marriage, fidelity, child-rearing, and money (in Plautus' *The Crock of Gold*, for example, the old miser Euclio is so obsessed with the treasure he's discovered buried in his house that he doesn't notice his daughter has been raped and is about to give birth)—but also on the last-minute resolution of these crises, which lies at the core of its huge influence on the subsequent Western tradition of comic drama.

As noted earlier, our view of Roman tragedy is no less partial than that of comedy, and although there was a continual tradition of Roman tragedy from the mid-3rd century BC, most of it is lost. Only ten tragedies survive, all of them from the later phase of its development at Rome and all ascribed to Seneca, although one of them, *Hercules on Mt Oeta*, is probably not by him, and a second, *Octavia*, our only extant example of a Roman historical drama, dealing with Nero's murder of his first wife, is certainly not by Seneca (who appears as a character in the play), since it refers to events after his death, including Nero's suicide. Though many scholars believe the eight genuine Senecan tragedies were written to be read or recited rather than performed on the stage, we can't be certain, and what matters in any case is the content and themes of the plays, which are highly revealing of their political and cultural context in the 40s–60s AD under the emperors Claudius and Nero.

Seneca had been banished in AD 41 by Claudius for alleged adultery with the former emperor Caligula's sister, but was recalled in 49 by Claudius' fourth wife, Agrippina, and appointed tutor to her 12-year-old son, Nero. When Nero became emperor in

54, Seneca became one of his closest advisers and gained enormous power and wealth, securing plum jobs for his friends and family as well. Implicated in the unsuccessful conspiracy to replace Nero, Seneca was forced to commit suicide in 65. Thus, much of Seneca's creative life was spent at the heart of imperial power and influence, and while it is easy to despise him for his hypocrisy—as a multi-millionaire, for example, who waxed philosophical about the unimportance of wealth, a stance that already prompted one contemporary to wonder, 'What sort of wisdom or maxims of philosophy enabled him within four years of royal favour to amass a fortune of 300 million sesterces?' (Tacitus, *Annals* 13.42)—he was nonetheless an acute observer of human frailties.

As in Greek tragedy, Seneca uses the monarchic world of Greek myth to reflect on the concerns of his day, not least the precarious political world created by one-man rule. Again and again we see how 'absolute power corrupts absolutely', and although there is no explicit reference to contemporary politics or criticism of Roman autocracy—that would have been asking for trouble in imperial Rome, and writers had already been killed for doing so under Tiberius—the pervasive atmosphere of looming and selfish evil that surrounds Seneca's powerful protagonists is bound to have resonated with contemporary readers or audiences. Politics aside, Seneca's tragedies are very much of their time in other respects: in their gruesome violence and baroque rhetoric, for example—his characters 'all seem to speak with the same voice, and at the top of it', to quote T. S. Eliot's caustic semi-exaggeration—or in their Stoic-influenced depiction of the chaos and suffering that ensue when human passions are not restrained. Finally, there is a striking metatheatrical awareness of being part of a long tragic tradition, as when Medea declares, as she rouses herself to take revenge on Jason by murdering their children, 'Now I am Medea' (*Medea* 910), or Oedipus, having discovered his crimes and blinded himself in shame, says 'This [blinded] face befits an Oedipus' (*Oedipus* 1003). Seneca's tragedies exerted a huge influence on English drama in the Elizabethan and Jacobean periods (especially Marlowe, Shakespeare, Jonson, and the many writers of revenge tragedy), and his focus on the violent and grotesque will be familiar to viewers of much modern drama, especially in its cinematic form.

In conclusion, theatre was an important part of community life in the ancient world: in the smallest towns, and at the very edges of the classical world, Greek and Roman settlers built theatres as basic elements of their culture. And no ancient genre is as vital in our time as Greek tragedy, which is performed all over the world, and still valued as a way to confront contemporary issues of war, imperialism, ethnicity, sexuality, and much else besides.

Chapter 5
Historiography

In this chapter we will look at how the Greeks and Romans conceived and wrote about their past. As we'll see, since investigation of the past is always moulded by the present, the historian's work tells us as much about his or her own period as it does about any other. We'll consider the influence of other genres (for example, epic, tragedy, and oratory) on the writing of history, and the extent to which ancient writers engaged in what we would recognize as historical research, rather than simply recasting earlier writers' versions of the past. We will also see how individual historians defended their claim to truth, and how the process of historical discovery could aim to explain many different things—Polybius on the rise of republican Rome, for example, or Sallust and Tacitus on its demise. Despite their shortcomings by modern standards of historical accuracy or impartiality, this chapter will also illustrate the great achievement of ancient historians, many of whom succeeded in gathering out of the way material and shaping it into a coherent narrative of complex events.

Historiography, the writing of 'history', defined as the scientific (i.e. evidence-based) investigation of the past, developed in Greece in the 5th century BC. But as we've seen in previous chapters, we can (with caution) use pre-historical literature such as epic or lyric as a guide to early Greek history. For the Greeks themselves, the

Homeric epics were the supreme examples of historical writing because they narrated the heroic origins of their society, and even pioneering historians like Herodotus and Thucydides, who took a more sceptical attitude to earlier (mythological) accounts of the past, especially those told by poets, considered Homer a valuable source of information on early Greek culture. Historians, both Greek and Roman, had to engage with epic, not least because they were dealing with very similar material: great wars and courageous acts, disastrous decisions and failures, survival and renewal. Indeed, from the very beginning history draws upon a wide range of other genres, from poetry in all its forms to philosophy and science, including geography and ethnography.

In the early historians we begin to see the idea that the mythical era is different from the historical era, and that the historian should focus on the latter, since only there can he check the evidence. There was no clear-cut dichotomy between myth and history, however, since people still took seriously their links to the mythical past, as when, for example, they boasted that their city was founded by a mythical hero or when aristocratic families claimed descent from the heroes themselves. Nonetheless, the earliest historians define themselves against myth, so that Herodotus emphasizes his focus on historical time, while Thucydides presents Herodotus and his predecessors as not sceptical enough about mythical or poetic accounts of the past, thereby boosting his own claim to accuracy and objectivity.

The earliest surviving historian, Herodotus, was heir to, and part of, a rational revolution that had its origins in the Greek cities of 6th-century BC Ionia (the west coast of modern Turkey), where thinkers began to investigate the natural world in a scientific manner, and to expose established traditions, including inherited accounts of the past, to sceptical inquiry. This critical engagement with the past is evident in the polemical opening to Hecataeus' *Genealogies*: 'Hecataeus of Miletus speaks thus: I write these things as they seem to me to be true. For the tales of the Greeks are, in my opinion, numerous and ridiculous' (fr. 1).

Herodotus has often been criticized for his credulity, but he is clear that his job is to find the best sources that he can and weigh them, not simply to believe all of them: 'I am obliged to report what I have been told, but I am certainly not obliged to believe it, and let that statement apply to my entire account' (7.152). Herodotus calls his work '*historiē*', which means 'inquiry' or 'research', a term that underlines his personal role as investigator: hence the emphasis throughout his work on travel (he speaks of inquiries throughout Greece, of course, but also in Italy, Egypt, southern Russia, Lebanon, and even Babylon on the Euphrates), speaking to local experts (via interpreters, when necessary), and seeing things for oneself (autopsy).

Some critics, ancient and modern, and influenced by Thucydides, have seen Herodotus' willingness to recount the marvellous and fantastic as undermining his claim to be a proper historian, but the division between scientific historian on the one hand, and credulous raconteur (or even liar) on the other, is too crude. We do better to recognize that Herodotus' combination of painstaking empirical research and rational analysis was an amazing achievement, especially given the resources then available to the budding historian and the risks of travel. He deserves his title as 'the father of history'.

The scope and aim of Herodotus' *Histories* are made clear in the programmatic opening sentence:

> This work displays the results of Herodotus of Halicarnassus' research (*historiē*), so that the things done by humankind do not fade out with the passage of time, nor the great and amazing achievements, some displayed by Greeks, some by barbarians, come to lose their fame, including (among other topics) why they went to war with one another. (1.1)

The word 'display' reminds us that Herodotus, like a poet, recited his work to Greek audiences (we might update and say 'This work publishes…'). His central subject will be the war between Greeks and barbarians (what we call the Persian Wars, 490–479 BC), but he immediately acknowledges the great achievements on both sides, and the importance of preserving their memory (another epic theme). Books 1–5 chart the expansion of the Persian empire, culminating in the two Persian invasions of Greece, first by king Darius (Book 6), defeated at Marathon in 490 BC, and the second much larger invasion under his son and successor Xerxes in 480–479 BC (Books 7–9), with its most famous battles at Thermopylae and Plataea on land, and Salamis at sea.

Throughout his *Histories*, Herodotus uses certain fundamental patterns of explanation, which not only give unity to his sprawling narrative, but also advertise the universal applicability and value of his work. Perhaps most basic is the principle of alternation, that is, the idea that 'human prosperity never remains in one place' (1.5), which Herodotus first illustrates by noting how cities that were once small are now great and those that were once great are now small (1.5). A second principle is the inevitable punishment of *hybris*, most strikingly illustrated in the excesses and failures of numerous Greek tyrants and barbarian kings, from king Croesus of Lydia in Book 1, whose foolish ambition leads him to overlook the ambiguity of the Delphic oracle's reply that 'if he leads an army against the Persians, he will destroy a great empire' (1.53—it turns out to be his own), through to a furious Xerxes having the waters of the Hellespont whipped, chained, and branded when his bridge is swept away (7.35). Finally, in the rise and fall of various rulers and peoples Herodotus sees a basic pattern of reciprocity, that is, 'good for good' and 'bad for bad', a system that not only propels change (as agents react to one another positively or negatively) but also, because it is supported by the gods, creates a sense of cosmic order.

As Herodotus travelled throughout the Mediterranean and beyond, he encountered a huge variety of societies with all sorts of customs and laws (the Greek word *nomoi* covers both), and he observes with great acuity that everyone thinks their own culture is best (3.38). Herodotus' awareness of the plurality of *nomoi* makes him wary of disrespecting the laws and customs of other peoples, but it does not make him a cultural relativist in the modern sense of abstaining from judgement, since he too thinks certain ways of life superior to others. This emerges most forcefully from his analysis of how the allied Greek city-states managed to defeat the military might of the Persian empire. For customs not only support civilized life, but also determine a culture's potential, and Herodotus sees in the superiority of Greek freedom over Persian autocracy the fundamental reason for the Greeks' remarkable victory (see Figure 5).

This is not to say that Herodotus denigrates barbarians—on the contrary, he is by fifth-century Greek standards unusually tolerant and open-minded, and he presents the east/west conflict not as a dichotomy of good vs evil but as a spectrum of cultural values, ranging from autocracy at one end to freedom of speech and action and equality before the law at the other. So there can be good foreign rulers and terrible Greek ones (tyrants), but his underlying analysis of the Persian Wars is that the Greeks' struggle to maintain freedom rightly triumphed over Persian attempts to impose one-man rule. At one point Herodotus even has the Persians debate the relative merits of monarchy, oligarchy, and democracy (3.80–3) and shows them *choosing* the autocratic form, with disastrous results, as their rulers succumb to the typical vices of sole power, including paranoia, unpredictability, disregard for ancestral law and custom, violation of women, and the murder of opponents.

Herodotus' huge range of interests contrasts with the narrower focus of Thucydides on politics, war, and economics, an orientation that had a huge influence on what was later considered the proper study of history, at least until the 20th century, when a new concern with social history, embracing (for

5. Interior of an Athenian red-figure drinking-cup by the Triptolemos Painter, *c*.480 BC, showing a Greek hoplite defeating a Persian warrior. Note the Persian's exotic costume (including striped trousers), which would have seemed decadent and bizarre to the ancient Greek viewer

example) gender and religion, returned the subject to a more Herodotean perspective. Thucydides' subject is the Peloponnesian War, fought between Athens and Sparta from 431 to 404 BC, which ended in Athens' defeat. Thucydides came from a wealthy Athenian family and was himself a general in the war, until he was exiled by the Athenians in 424 for failing to secure the northern Greek city of Amphipolis from the Spartans, led by Brasidas. Thucydides reports his own failure and exile, but also emphasizes throughout the great military skill of Brasidas (implying that to lose to him did not make Thucydides a bad soldier), and spins his exile positively by saying it enabled him to gather evidence from both sides (5.26). Thucydides' banishment may also have influenced his contempt for most of the Athenian politicians and generals who came to prominence after the city's leading statesman Pericles, whom Thucydides greatly admired, died from the plague in 429. Though Thucydides lived to see the end of the war, he died before completing his account of it, and his history ends in the middle of a sentence discussing the events of 411. Nonetheless, Thucydides' conception of the war as a whole, including the reasons for Athens' defeat, emerges from the surviving eight books, whose analysis of the machinations of *Realpolitik*, and of human behaviour under the pressures of war, has never been surpassed.

Thucydides was admired already in antiquity as the foremost historian and he has been hailed in modern times as the inventor of scientific and objective history, which is very much how he presents himself in the opening sections of his work, where he sets out his methods, contrasting his accuracy, thorough investigation of sources, and understanding of historical causation with the shoddy techniques of his predecessors. They are 'poets' and 'story-tellers' rather than historians (1.21), and whereas (Thucydides claims) their goal is entertainment, his is a true understanding of the past that will be of permanent value:

> The absence of the mythical element will perhaps make my work rather unentertaining in recitation; but if it is judged useful by those who want a clear understanding both of past events and of those future events which because of the human condition will be similar or nearly so, I shall be satisfied. My work is composed as a possession for all time rather than a competition piece to be heard for the moment. (1.22)

As this passage makes clear, Thucydides is confident that the audience (or reader) will learn from his history of the Peloponnesian War how the world works. As in epic, war is presented by Thucydides as a testing ground of human character, displaying courage, ingenuity, and resilience, but also selfishness, cruelty, and dehumanization. The Athenians' disastrous attempt to invade and control Sicily in 415–413 BC, which ends with every one of their soldiers either killed or enslaved, is paradigmatic of the risks of war in general, especially the dangers of overconfidence and not knowing one's enemy. The horrors of armed conflict are particularly graphic in the case of civil war, where a community turns against itself, resulting in moral and social collapse. Thucydides' account of the civil war on the island of Corcyra (modern Corfu) is a profound analysis of 'human nature' (a key element in Thucydides' historical imagination) under the pressure of violence and social breakdown:

> In times of peace and prosperity both states and individuals follow higher standards because they are not forced into situations where they must act against their will; but war, by taking away the easy satisfaction of daily needs, is a violent teacher, and assimilates most people's tempers to their present circumstances. (3.82)

Just as he depicts the glories and the cruelties of war, so Thucydides also analyses both the appeal and the risks of imperialism, which he sees as a natural consequence of the human urge for power and status. The Athenians justify their empire in the bluntest terms: 'it has always been a rule that the weaker should be subject to the stronger' (1.76). And Thucydides presents Pericles himself glorying in the extent of the Athenians' dominion over other Greek states and the dynamism of their imperial spirit (2.64). However, Thucydides also makes clear the inherent danger and instability of empire, not only because it is subject to the unpredictability of war, which is necessary to win and maintain it, but also because it excites fear and envy, as when (in Thucydides' analysis) the expansion of Athens' power leads to the Spartans' declaration of war. He also portrays the victims of empire, as when the island of Melos attempts to remain neutral in the war: the Athenians put all the men of the island to death, and enslave the women and children. As this and other episodes show, the human struggle for power and advantage may be inevitable, but power once achieved can also be misused. (Appropriately, the destruction of Melos in 416 BC is immediately followed by the Athenians' disastrous attempt to conquer Sicily.)

Thucydides was a conservative aristocrat, who was wary of democracy: he says of the oligarchy of 5,000 select citizens that controlled the city for a brief period in 411 BC that 'the Athenians appear to have been well governed, at least for the first time in my lifetime' (8.97). He conceded that democracy worked well when it was led by one man, Pericles—'what was nominally a democracy became in his hands government by the first citizen' (2.65)—and he thought this proper balance between the people and its betters was corrupted by Pericles' successors, whose personal rivalries and shortsighted appeal to the whims of the people he saw as key reasons for Athens' defeat.

But despite these and other biases, Thucydides' analysis of leadership remains compelling: the statesman needs intelligence and foresight if he is to react to the unexpected (a constant feature of politics and war) with good planning and thus avert disaster. So while we should resist the temptation to take Thucydides' supremely intelligent account of 5th-century BC Greek history as definitive, his work was nonetheless a huge development in historiography in its striving for accuracy and explanation based on careful observation (he was the first to write the history of his own times), criteria of probability (so that he can reconstruct what an Athenian general is likely to have said before the final showdown in Sicily, for example), and a comprehensive, if rather bleak, analysis of human motivation.

Of the many Greek historians who wrote during the Hellenistic period (the standard modern edition lists over 850 of them), no complete texts survive, but we have a substantial portion of the most important of them, Polybius, whose theme is the rise of Rome in the years 220–146 BC to become the major power in the

Mediterranean world. No historian writing in this period could ignore Rome's remarkable expansion, and Polybius' aim is both to decribe and explain Rome's success. He writes for Romans (whose political elite knew Greek) as well as for his fellow Greeks, and his goal is didactic as well as historical, since all readers could learn from his account of what moral qualities and what kind of constitution made Rome's triumph possible. He devotes an entire book (6) to the Roman state and its institutions, continuing Herodotus' focus on different types of constitution (monarchy, aristocracy/oligarchy, and democracy) and their consequences, but whereas Herodotus had foregrounded the hazards of monarchy and the benefits of democracy, Polybius sees in Rome's tripartite constitution, which used elements of all three forms, the main reason for Rome's success—together with, as he notes, the all-conquering Juggernaut of the Roman army.

Strikingly, however, we also find in Polybius, at this early stage in the development of Rome's empire, an emphasis on the danger of corruption and decadence that comes in empire's wake (18.35, 31.25, 35.4). This idea of Roman decadence and decline is a leitmotif of Roman literature, especially Roman historiography. Several factors encouraged such a narrative: the exceptional scale of Roman power; the traditional nature of Roman culture, with its emphasis on *mos maiorum* ('ancestral custom') and suspicion of the new; and not least the actual destruction of the republic in civil war and its descent into dictatorship.

The influence of Greek historiography on Roman is considerable, and the first native Roman historian, Fabius Pictor, working in the late 3rd century BC, even wrote in Greek, as did his early successors. The first to write Roman history in Latin prose was the elder Cato, whom we met in Chapter 1 as a champion of down-to-earth Romanness in opposition to sophisticated, too-clever Greeks. Cato began writing his *Origins* around 168 BC and was still working on it at his death in 149. Though only fragments survive, we can already see in the *Origins* many of the distinctive features of Roman historiography.

First, as its title implies, Cato's work tells the story of Rome and Italy 'from the beginning' down to his own day (Cato himself is a character in his history), which became a popular format for Roman historians, who often began their narratives with the arrival of the legendary Aeneas in Italy (as did Fabius Pictor and Cato) or with the later foundation of Rome by Romulus and Remus in 753 BC. Second, virtually no written sources were available for early Roman history, and so in dealing with this period Cato is relying on folk memory and 'historical myths' and adapting them to suit his time. This is not to say that Roman historians were not committed to the truth—that certainly remained the ideal, and it is a standard claim of Roman historians to be free from bias—but they faced huge problems in finding reliable sources, especially for early periods, and they rarely questioned the accuracy of the previous histories that were generally the basis for theirs. Thus the writing of history owed as much (and in many cases more) to poetry and rhetoric as to long hours slogging away in the senatorial archives. Third, Cato thinks history should teach useful lessons, and the moral and didactic nature of history is particularly prominent in Roman culture. Thus Roman historians often focus on what can be learned from exemplary figures and events of the past, both good and bad. Related to this is Cato's emphasis on the common good: he does not name individual magistrates or commanders, thereby eliding their personal glory and stressing instead their service to Rome.

The first Roman historian whose works survive complete is Sallust, whose *War against Catiline* and *War against Jugurtha*, both written in the late 40s BC, take the form of monographs on discrete episodes in recent history: the Roman aristocrat Catiline's failed conspiracy to overthrow the republic in 63–62 BC and Rome's war with Jugurtha, king of Numidia in north Africa, in 111–104 BC. Sallust sees in both struggles the symptoms of a pervasive and irreparable degeneration among the ruling Roman elite, whose obsession with wealth and power is corrupting public life, so that they (among other dangerous acts) misuse the Roman army (as in *Jugurtha*), or exploit the desperation of the poor (as in *Catiline*), to further their own personal ambitions. Despite the rather schematic moralizing, Sallust's spiky style and disenchanted view of Roman power politics was widely enjoyed, and he was a huge influence on Tacitus, the most profound investigator of Roman history.

Sallust fought for Caesar in the civil war of the early 40s BC and, as it happens, the only other 'historical' works to survive complete from the republican period are Caesar's own *Gallic War* and *Civil War*. In seven books Caesar describes his conquest of Gaul (58–51 BC), including two expeditions to Britain in 55 and 54 BC, in the second of which he forced the payment of tribute from Cassivellaunus, king of the shaggy hordes of Hertfordshire. Caesar presents the conquest of Gaul as a legitimate response to requests from the Gallic tribes themselves, to repel attacks from one another or from German invaders, thus masking its true purpose in boosting Caesar's campaign coffers (to fund bribery back in Rome) and training his legions for the power struggle ahead. His three books on the civil war emphasize his patriotism, clemency, and desire for peace, and counter his senatorial enemies' image of him as a dangerous revolutionary by depicting himself as a defender of the republic and its traditions. He refers to himself in the third-person throughout ('On receipt of this news, Caesar ordered the army to advance', etc.), creating an air of objectivity, but actually foregrounding his own authority and skill.

Obviously, both works of Caesar are closer to propaganda than to history, but it's still a rare occurrence today to find the memoirs of a general or politician that aren't largely self-justification. These texts may be shaped by Caesar's political ambitions, but they are still fascinating for what they reveal about the tactics of one of the most influential figures of the ancient world, and during one of the most turbulent and brutal periods in European history. Caesar's plain and clear writing style, which is geared to seduce the reader into accepting his version of events as the unvarnished truth, has also made him the bane of schoolchildren beginning Latin for centuries—who, if they remember anything of their lessons, know that 'The whole of Gaul is divided into three parts...' (1.1)—thereby doing much to shape the modern view of ruthless, militaristic Romans.

In contrast to Sallust and Caesar's focus on episodes in recent or contemporary history, the massive 142-book work of Livy, entitled *From the Founding of the City*, spanned the whole of Roman history from its origins down to 9 BC. Only 35 books survive: 1-10 (753-293 BC) and 21-45 (218-167 BC). Livy arranges his material year-by-year, and his coverage gets more detailed as he gets closer to his own time, where he has more literary sources to draw on: thus by Book 21, where Rome is at war with Hannibal (218 BC), he has already covered well over 500 years. Like Polybius (one of his major sources), Livy's aim was to chronicle the expansion of Roman power and illustrate the virtues that underpinned its success. Livy makes clear in his Preface the purpose and value of history:

> This indeed is an especially healthy and fruitful benefit of the study of history, that you see models of every type of behaviour set up as on a perspicuous memorial: from these you can choose for yourself and for your country what to imitate, and also what to avoid, whether disgraceful in its beginnings or disgraceful in its outcome.
>
> (*Preface* 10)

History as a series of good and bad examples sounds rather monotonous, and what saves Livy's didactic project from dullness is his brilliance as a story-teller, capable of creating convincing characters and dramatic narratives. Many of the tales of Roman history which Livy handles were already well known to his audience—ranging from famous episodes of heroism and self-sacrifice (e.g. Horatius Cocles defending the bridge over the Tiber) to those of tyrannical cruelty (e.g. the rape of Lucretia, which led to the abolition of the monarchy and the establishment of the republic)—but he makes them suspenseful and gripping, and the Romans' enjoyment of his dramatic historical style might be compared with our own pleasure in reading historical novelists such as Hilary Mantel or William Boyd—with the bonus that Livy preserves much historical detail that would otherwise be lost.

It is a particular shame that the later books of Livy do not survive, since it would be fascinating to see how he presented Augustus and his claim to be the restorer of the republic. What is clear is that the change from republic to principate—*princeps* meaning 'first citizen', a euphemism for the absolute power of the emperor—had a profound impact on the writing of history. Under Augustus' successor, Tiberius, the historian Cremutius Cordus was charged with treason for writing a pro-republican account of the civil wars: the cowed senate condemned Cremutius, his books were burnt, and he starved himself to death (AD 25). By contrast, the works of pro-imperial historians and moralists such as Velleius Paterculus and Valerius Maximus are marked by sycophantic flattery of Tiberius, and their toeing of the establishment line helps explain why the imperial system lasted so long. Fortunately, however, a critical account of the principate has survived, and it is written by the greatest Roman historian of all.

Tacitus wrote his historical works, the *Histories* and the *Annals*, in the early 2nd century AD during the reigns of Trajan and Hadrian, but he was savvy enough not to write contemporary history—now a risky undertaking, unless one was content largely to flatter. Instead he covered in his *Histories* the years AD 69–96, from the death of Nero and the 'Year of the Four Emperors' (Galba, Otho, Vitellius, and Vespasian) down to the death of the repressive Domitian. Tacitus depicts the chaos of the civil wars and the bloody emergence of yet another imperial dynasty, Vespasian and his sons, Titus and Domitian. But it is the *Annals*, written after the *Histories* but dealing with the earlier period of the Julio-Claudian dynasty, from the accession of Tiberius to the suicide of Nero, which offer the most penetrating and censorious picture of the imperial system and its effects on both the emperor and his subjects.

Each of the three emperors handled in the surviving books of the *Annals* is presented as disastrously flawed: Tiberius deceptive and sadistic, Claudius a weak-minded cuckold and a pedant, and Nero a mother-killing psycho with a fondness for showing off his imagined talents as actor, singer, or chariot-racer. (Sadly, the books on the notoriously depraved and brutal emperor Caligula are lost.) Thanks to Tacitus it is impossible to think of imperial Rome without seeing Nero fiddling—or rather singing to the lyre—as Rome burns (*Annals* 15.39). But as well as offering vivid portrayals of deranged autocrats, Tacitus also damns his fellow members of the governing classes for conniving in their own servility. The opening description of their reaction to Tiberius' accession is emblematic of the work as a whole:

> But at Rome consuls, senators, knights rushed into slavery. The more eminent men were, so the more hypocritical and eager they were, and with carefully composed looks, so as not to seem happy at the death of one ruler or sad at the beginning of another's reign, they mixed tears, joy, grief, and sycophancy. (*Annals* 1.7)

Their spinelessness sickens even the emperor himself:

> The story goes that whenever he left the Senate House Tiberius used to exclaim in Greek, 'Men fit for slavery!' Clearly, even he, who opposed public freedom, was tired of such degrading submission in his slaves. (*Annals* 3.65)

Thus, although Tacitus laments the loss of republican freedoms (especially for senators like himself), he is not so naïve as to forget the political ambitions and factional rivalries that led to the collapse of the republic, and he recognizes the inevitability of one-man rule if the alternative is civil war. However, as the 'Year of the Four Emperors' shows, the principate itself is no guarantee against civil war, and imperial Rome continues to suffer from the ambition, corruption, and violence that led to its creation.

At the beginning of the *Annals* Tacitus makes the historian's conventional claim to impartiality, saying that he will treat the imperial succession from Augustus onwards 'without anger or bias' (*sine ira et studio*, 1.1). But his personal conviction that the principate corrupts both the ruler and the ruled makes itself felt throughout his narrative. Among ancient historians Tacitus thus ranks alongside Herodotus for the intelligence and insight with which he analyses the damage done by autocratic forms of government to both individual and society. He had no match in later historiography—or biography, a genre which, because of its focus on one man, especially on his character and use of power, became popular under the empire. Tacitus' response to that empire is not only a masterpiece of historical narrative, but also a testament to the power of truth in the face of political oppression which has lost none of its force or relevance.

Chapter 6
Oratory

The skill of effective and persuasive speech plays a part in every human community, and the ability to speak well was always highly prized in Greek and Roman society. This chapter will examine the reasons for oratory's importance in the classical world and how it developed to meet the changing demands of speakers and audiences. The rules and techniques underpinning effective communication were known in the ancient world as 'rhetoric', and learning the art of rhetoric was the backbone of higher education for Greeks and Romans from the 5th century BC onwards. Strictly speaking, our focus here is on oratory rather than rhetoric, that is, on the surviving speeches rather than the technical rules underlying them, though both are for obvious reasons intertwined. Oratory is perhaps the ancient genre least appreciated in our own time, tainted as it is by the (pejoratively charged) 'rhetoric' of politicians et al., but it contains some of the finest examples of Greek and Latin prose, and the surviving speeches illuminate many essential features of Greek and Roman society.

We see the importance of oratory already in early Greek epic, long before the age of technical treatises and formal training, since Homer's ideal hero is a 'speaker of words' as well as a 'doer of deeds'. But it is in the democratic city-states of 5th-century BC

Sicily and Athens that we see oratory blossom into a major and essential form of mass persuasion. Whether in the democratic assembly or the law-courts, the speaker's success depended on his—and it was always his, since women were considered political and legal 'minors'—ability to persuade a large body of his peers to vote in his favour. (The assembly held many thousands, while an Athenian jury comprised several hundred citizens, the exact number depending on the type of case.) Democratic communities such as Athens took great pride in the individual citizen's right to freedom of speech, but that freedom came with the responsibility to participate directly in politics and to represent oneself in the courts, albeit with the help of a speech-writer, if necessary. With (in some legal cases) the speaker's life or livelihood on the line, and with no judges or professional lawyers to guide opinion, the individual's ability to win over a mass audience was crucial, and it is no surprise that the surviving speeches, political as well as legal, use emotional appeals as much as reasoned argument.

As in modern democratic societies, pride in freedom of speech co-existed with suspicion of the slick talker and anxiety about the unscrupulous use of oratory. Critics of democracy, such as the conservative Thucydides or the reactionary Plato, pointed to the people (*dēmos*) being swayed by self-interested speakers (or demagogues), but the Athenians wisely calculated that the risk of deception was a price worth paying for political equality. Or one could always point to the problem that skilled rhetoric can sway a jury to acquit when the facts of the case suggest otherwise, but we have the same situation today: everyone knows a good lawyer or barrister makes a difference, and juries or judges still have to be persuaded. Plato's odd-ball rejection of democratic rhetoric fell on deaf ears, and the most influential analysis of Greek oratory was written by Plato's more pragmatic pupil, Aristotle, who recognized its legitimate role in public life. It is to Aristotle that we owe the schematic but useful division of oratory into three broad types: deliberative, forensic, and display.

Deliberative oratory was usually directed at political assemblies and might be compared to a modern parliamentary speech. There were no political parties in the ancient world and politics was propelled by individuals. The successful political speaker needed the ability to improvise, since he won't have known exactly how a debate would develop. Key facts and passages could be memorized, but the speaker who could not think on his feet would not last long. Since plaintiffs and defendants spoke on their own behalf, the speaker in forensic or law-court oratory was usually an amateur, who relied on an expert to write his speech (if he could afford one), and it was an essential measure of the professional orator's skill that his speech create a persona for his client which would win him the case. It was not acceptable to read from a text in court, so the speaker had to rely on memory, but again a skilled speech-writer was expected to create the illusion of impromptu delivery. The courts were also an arena for political feuds, with charges of fraud and misconduct of various kinds flying around, and there was always work for good orators. Finally, display or ceremonial oratory marked important events in the life of the community, the most solemn being the genre of the funeral speech, where the city-state honoured those citizens who had died fighting on its behalf. Such speeches assert the common values of speaker and audience, bolstering and celebrating their shared identity.

So let's consider some examples. The law-court speech by Lysias entitled *On the Murder of Eratosthenes* is one of the most fascinating to have survived, replete as it is with details of everyday family life in classical Athens. The defendant, Euphiletus, is on trial for killing Eratosthenes, a fellow citizen, but (he argues) since he caught Eratosthenes *in flagrante delicto* with his wife, he was justified in killing him on the spot. The speech is a historian's dream, since it tells us a great deal about a range of social and legal issues, from the policing of female behaviour and concerns about adultery and legitimacy through to the shape and layout of Athenian houses. But its literary skill is also outstanding, and Lysias' deceptively simple and clear style creates a persona for the speaker which is perfectly fitted to winning the case. Here, for example, Euphiletus describes his wife's suspicious behaviour and his innocent reaction:

> After a while, gentlemen, I came home unexpectedly from the
> country. After dinner the baby started to cry and howl, as he was
> being deliberately tormented by the servant-girl to behave like this,
> because the man was in the house—I discovered all of this afterwards.
> So I told my wife to go and give the baby the breast to stop him
> crying. At first she refused, as if she were glad to see me back again
> after so long. When I began to get angry and told her to go, she said,
> 'Oh yes, so you can have a go at the young servant-girl here! You've
> grabbed at her before when you were drunk.' (Lysias, 1.11–12)

The narrative casts Euphiletus as naïve and trusting, whereas his wife is deceptive, turning the household servants against their master, and even using her baby to further her own lust: every word is geared to generate the maximum indignation in a jury of male Athenian citizens.

Euphiletus' artfully simple language suggests an honest, not too clever, plain-speaking man, but the style can also rise to grander tones, as when the defendant recalls his final words to the adulterer:

> And he himself admitted his crime, but he begged and beseeched
> me not to kill him, but to exact a sum of money. But I replied, 'It is
> not I who shall be killing you, but the law of the city, which you
> transgressed and regarded as less important than your pleasures,
> choosing to commit this foul offence against my wife and my
> children rather than to obey the laws and behave decently.' (1.25–6)

This is a masterly tactic, exploiting the Athenian jury's pride in their legal system and its superiority to vendetta violence. By declaring to the jurors 'I did not kill Eratosthenes, your laws did',

Euphiletus presents himself not as an angry husband meting out a brutal and premeditated revenge, but as a just instrument of the Athenians' laws, carrying out instant punishment on their behalf.

Demosthenes was regarded in antiquity as the greatest Greek orator, and his efforts to rouse and to advise the Athenians in their struggle with the rising power of Philip of Macedon resulted in some of the most brilliant political oratory ever written. In the first of his appropriately entitled *Philippics*, delivered in 351 BC, Demosthenes mixes inspiring (and shaming) remembrance of past Athenian glories with sarcastic criticism of his audience's current timidity and slowness to react:

> You, men of Athens, have unsurpassed resources—warships, infantry, cavalry, financial revenues—but to this very day you have never used them as you should, and you wage war with Philip in the same way as barbarians fight in a boxing-match. When one of them is hit, he always clutches where he was hit; if he gets a blow on the other side, there go his hands: he neither knows nor cares how to put up a guard or face his opponent. (*Philippics* 1.40)

Like untrained, foreign boxers, the Athenians keep moving their troops to places that Philip has already hit, rather than to where he's going to hit. All of Demosthenes' speeches dealing with the rise of Macedon depict Demosthenes himself, not surprisingly, as a heroic champion of freedom in a war against tyranny. Since we know his struggle was in vain, as Athens fell under Philip and then his son Alexander the Great's monarchy (and its successors), the speeches have a wistful as well as a rousing quality, like epitaphs on the end of democracy.

The speeches of the Athenian orators were widely read by members of the Roman elite as part of their education, which focused to a large extent on models of rhetoric capable of preparing the Roman citizen for the duties and challenges of public life. As with the writing of history, the elder Cato plays an important role in the origins of Roman oratory, though only fragments of his speeches remain. He insisted on speaking in Latin to the Athenian assembly, though he knew Greek, making the point that Latin was now the dominant language in the Mediterranean world. And his famously pithy advice on how to be an effective speaker, 'get a grip on the subject, the words will follow' (*rem tene, verba sequentur*), builds on the contrast between wordy, deceptive Greeks and direct, no-waffle Romans that Cato was adept at exploiting for his own political ends. The surviving fragments display his punchy style, and the aptness of his themes: 'Thieves of private property spend their lives in prisons and chains; public thieves in gold and purple' (*Speeches* fr. 224).

As in Greece, speaking well was essential to all areas of Roman public life, especially in the law-courts and politics (whether addressing public meetings or the more exclusive senate), but also in military, diplomatic, and religious contexts. In the sphere of law-court oratory, Roman practice differed from the Greek in allowing an advocate to speak on one's behalf, and such orators had to be (or at least give the impression of being) figures of standing and authority in Roman society. But the advocate's persona was also flexible, and so we see in Cicero, the greatest Roman orator (and the only orator of the republican period from whom we have complete speeches), a constant effort to present himself in terms that suit the needs of the particular case, from the outraged Roman traditionalist of *Against Piso*, for example, who attacks his target for *inter alia* military incompetence, provincial corruption, debauchery, and poor (Epicurean) philosophy, to the avuncular apologist of *In Defence of Caelius*, who excuses his client's shocking lifestyle by the classic 'argument' of 'boys will be boys' and by portraying him as the innocent victim of a seductive and immoral older woman. Cicero's renowned adaptability led to Catullus' ambiguous description of him as *optimus omnium patronus* (Poem 49), which can be read as 'the best advocate of all', but also as 'the best advocate-of-all'—in other

Classical Literature

94

words, as an orator without principle who will represent anyone as long as it furthers his own career.

In the previous chapter we saw how the historian Sallust treated the Roman aristocrat Catiline's failed conspiracy to overthrow the republic. Cicero viewed his part in foiling the conspiracy during the last months of his consulship in 63 BC as the highlight of his political career (see Figure 6). Although Cicero was exiled five years later for executing some of the conspirators without a trial, he never ceased to celebrate or justify his actions, even writing a poem about his consulship, of which scraps survive (unless they're a parody of the original, which was ridiculed on publication), the most extensive being 'O what a happy fate for the Roman state was the date of my consulate!' (*O fortunatam natam me consule Romam*).

Fortunately, Cicero was much better at oratory, and his four Catilinarian orations, which are revised versions of the original speeches, written up by Cicero in 60 BC to justify his controversial conduct three years before, offer a vivid depiction of the factional politics and violence that led to the destruction of the republic in

6. Cesare Maccari, *Cicero Denounces Catiline*, painted for the Senate of the Italian Republic (1888)

civil war. The rhetoric is grand and unsubtle: Cicero is the selfless defender of the fatherland, Catiline its treacherous and perverted enemy, and Rome herself is personified, pleading with Catiline to leave her in peace (1.18). Cicero's monochrome analysis may not be alive to the underlying institutional weaknesses that have led to the ambition and chaos of his times, and his self-glorification becomes tiresome, but his attempt to justify the execution of the conspirators in the name of freedom and national security remains as relevant as ever.

We see another side of Cicero's talents as an orator in the forensic speech *In Defence of Caelius*, delivered in 56 BC, the year after Cicero returned from exile. His client Marcus Caelius Rufus had been accused of seditious violence, but this serious charge, connected to the assassination of Egyptian diplomats on an embassy to Rome, is completely sidestepped by Cicero, who focuses his efforts instead on assassinating the character of Clodia, one of the prosecution's witnesses, who had claimed that Caelius borrowed money from her to buy poison. It's one thing not to get bogged down in legal technicalities—Demosthenes was famously good at avoiding this, since he knew such details could bore the audience—but quite another to ignore the real charges, as Cicero does here, concentrating instead on depicting Clodia as a whore, who also sleeps with her brother Clodius—coincidentally, or rather not, the same man who sponsored the bill for Cicero's exile. In Cicero's version of events, Clodia seduced the naïve and innocent young Caelius, but he eventually left her in disgust, so that now she, the spurned lover, is out for revenge.

If that sounds like a familiar plot, it's because it is, and Cicero has deliberately cast his speech as if it were a theatrical entertainment, mixing references to tragedy, comedy, and mime in order to entertain and misdirect his audience. Thus Clodia is compared to the rejected and vengeful Medea, Caelius' youthful excess is excused by contrasting the reactions of two fathers from Roman comedy (one stern and unattractive, the other lenient and sympathetic), and the alleged plot to deliver the poison descends into farce with a slapstick scene set in the public baths. Cicero's deft use of humour here and elsewhere defies his unfair reputation as a pompous windbag, and his strategy of comic misdirection paid off, as Caelius was acquitted. (Caelius cannily backed Caesar in the civil wars to come, but was killed in 48 BC during an attempted rebellion against him.)

Cicero's political speeches, including his *Philippics* against Mark Antony (the title evoking Demosthenes' defence of Greek freedom), are the best and final examples of oratory being used to influence political life in Rome. Cicero was killed by Antony's men in December 43 BC, and his head and hands were cut off and nailed to the speaker's platform in the forum, symbolizing the end of free political oratory as the republican system continued its descent into one-man rule. Oratory remained an essential part of education and public life under the principate in both Latin- and Greek-speaking communities, whether in law-courts, local councils, or various civic contexts, and performing orators enjoyed popularity and prestige throughout the empire. But the loss of political liberty took its toll.

Pliny's *Panegyric*, an expanded version of the speech he gave in the senate thanking the emperor Trajan for his 'election' to the consulship in AD 100, fulfils its brief of praising the emperor by contrasting him with his tyrannical predecessor, Domitian: 'Nowhere should we flatter him as a divinity and a god; we are not talking of a tyrant but of a fellow citizen, not of an overlord but of a parent' (2). Power, Pliny implies, no longer needs flattery—a remarkable sentiment in a eulogy that fills 81 pages. All the surviving Latin panegyrics of the emperors, though nauseous to our taste, are valuable for what they reveal about how power was wielded in the imperial system—and prompt us to ask how we would behave under an autocratic government.

So although the techniques of rhetoric were criticized in antiquity, and people recognized that oratory could be abused (as could any other skill), they also saw its importance as an essential part of public life, and the ideal of free speech was prized, not least because of the many threats it faced. Finally, as other chapters of this book make clear, oratory's fundamental role in society is also shown by its prominence in a range of literary texts, where it leaves its mark on almost every genre of classical literature, from (for example) the extended speeches of epic, drama, and history to the highly rhetorical performances of satire.

Chapter 7
Pastoral

This chapter will examine the invention of pastoral poetry in the urban metropolis of Alexandria in Hellenistic Egypt, showing how the genre's literary sophistication and nostalgia for rural simplicity appealed to learned city-dwelling poets and their readers. We will also consider how the genre was transformed at Rome, as contemporary politics and civil war enter the pastoral world, disrupting its potential as an idealized retreat from, or alternative to, city life. As one would expect in an essentially agricultural society, poets had always written about the countryside, and we can see pastoral elements in Greek literature long before Theocritus formalized the genre in works written at the Alexandrian court in the early 3rd century BC. We saw in Chapter 2, for example, how the early epic poet Hesiod portrayed the countryside as a place of honest toil in his didactic *Works and Days*, while the emphasis on the countryside as a place of beauty and repose, one of the hallmarks of pastoral as a genre, is already present in the age-old motif of the *locus amoenus*, or 'pleasant place', which we find throughout Greek literature from Homer onwards, especially in the *Odyssey*'s portrayal of the fertile lands of the Phaeacians and Cyclopes, the islands of the beguiling Calypso and Circe, and Odysseus' beloved Ithaca.

But although Theocritus was not the first author to write about rural life, he was the first to compose a group of poems focusing on 'bucolic song' (*boukolos* meaning 'cowherd')—that is, on the musical performances of herdsmen in rural settings—thereby securing his status as the founder of pastoral. Theocritus' eight bucolic poems are only one part of a wider and varied oeuvre, but they have always been the most popular and influential of his works. Thus the ancients gave the name 'idylls' (or *eidyllia*, meaning 'vignettes') to all his poems, but it is the term's application to the pastoral poems in particular that gives us the modern sense of 'idyll' or 'idyllic' as a space of rural beauty and tranquillity. The to us quaint scenario of cowherds, shepherds, and goatherds performing, or competing in, music and song draws on the reality of the ancient rural world, where solitary herdsmen sang or played wooden pipes to allay boredom and, should they meet a fellow worker out on the hills, might play or sing together, or in competition with one another. So Theocritus is building on a genuine feature of rural life, but has extensively stylized and idealized it to create a highly artificial pastoral world. For unlike Hesiod's realistically sweaty account of rural labour, these pastoral figures are more concerned with showcasing their musical abilities or lamenting unrequited love (and often the two go together).

Theocritus uses the metre of epic to depict non-heroic content—herdsmen speaking in a rustic Doric dialect, even at times indulging in obscene banter—creating an effect of artful incongruity aimed at delighting his sophisticated Alexandrian audience with its originality and artifice. Moreover, the effect is not to sneer at these 'rustics' but to share in their overwhelming enjoyment of poetry and song. This is well conveyed by the opening lines of the first poem, where the shepherd Thyrsis addresses an unnamed goatherd:

THYRSIS
Sweet is the music of that pine tree's whisper, goatherd,
there by the springs, and sweet too is your

piping; you will carry off the second prize after Pan.
If he chooses the horned billy-goat, you will have the nanny.
And if he takes the nanny as his prize, to you falls
the kid; and a kid's meat is good until you milk her.

GOATHERD
Shepherd, your song sounds sweeter than the resounding
water that pours down from the high rock.
If the Muses take the ewe as their prize,
you will have a stall-fed lamb; and if it pleases them
to have the lamb, you will carry off the ewe. (1.1–11)

In other words, just as Hesiod's *Works and Days* and Virgil's
Georgics are only ostensibly about agriculture (see Chapter 2), so
Theocritean pastoral is more about poetry and its place within the
poetic tradition than it is about goats or lambs, no matter how
valuable. Such 'metapoetry'—that is, poetic reflection on the
creation and value of poetry itself—is found in other ancient
genres (for example, in lyric, comedy, love elegy, or satire), but it is
particularly important to pastoral, whose rural workers are at the
same time creators of song.

This is clearest in poem 7, entitled 'The Harvest Festival', whose
narrator, Simichidas, is himself a composer and performer of bucolic
poetry. The poem tells how Simichidas met the goatherd, Lycidas,
some years before on the island of Cos. Even before they compete in
song Lycidas promises Simichidas his own staff as a prize:

I shall present you with my staff because you are
a sapling created by Zeus entirely for truth.
How I hate the builder who strives
to raise his house as high as Mt Oromedon's peak,
and those cocks of the Muses who waste their energy
crowing in vain against Homer, Chios' bard. (7.43–8)

Theocritus here echoes the aesthetic of his fellow Alexandrian
poet Callimachus, whose preference for small-scale, erudite poetry

also entailed the rejection of bombastic, sub-Homeric epic (see Chapter 1). Moreover, Lycidas' gift of his staff creates a scene that is evocative of previous poetic initiations, as when the Muses appear to Hesiod while he tends his sheep on Mt Helicon and inspire him to become a poet (*Theogony* 22–34). The combination of literary manifesto and Simichidas' investiture as a poet has led many to take the narrator as a symbol for Theocritus himself, but things are not so simple, and there is humour at Simichidas' expense, since his cocky self-assurance about his talents as a bucolic *poet* contrasts with the goatherd Lycidas' genuine connection to the countryside and its traditions.

Lycidas' more convincing connection to the rural world is part of pastoral's wider contrast between the simplicity and authenticity of country life on the one hand, and the sophistication and fakery of metropolitan life on the other—even though, paradoxically, this contrast is expressed in learned poetry written by and for city-dwelling poets and their audiences. It is no coincidence that pastoral developed in a period of urban expansion and in the jazziest of Hellenistic cities, Alexandria. Modern parallels spring to mind: the *Naturphilosophie* of the German Romantics, for example, and their influence via Coleridge on Wordsworth and the other Lake writers, all during the boom of the Industrial Revolution in northern Europe (*c.*1760–1820). So the idea of the rural world as a refuge from urban life, still at work in our own utopian fantasies of escape to the country, has a long history, and can seduce even pre-industrial societies.

Ancient pastoral exploits such an idealizing view of the countryside—the creation of city-dwellers rather than people who live and work on the land, where low-class but contented workers enjoy mystical communion with the natural world—but Theocritus also exposes how artificial and utopian it all is. For in poking fun at the overly smooth bucolic poet Simichidas, Theocritus makes clear that this is entertainment for an urban audience, prompting us to ask what city people actually know about the country, and to question their nostalgia for an older, simpler way of life that is now threatened or lost, but which in reality never actually existed. Theocritus' ironic distance from the bucolic ideal thus saves his work from the cloying sentimentality that pervades not only the *Lament for Adonis* by his early successor, Bion, but also many texts and paintings of the modern European pastoral tradition. Finally, Theocritean pastoral's focus on country life is also part of a wider trend towards 'realism' in Hellenistic literature and art (such idyllic scenes became very popular in later Roman wall-painting as an adornment to expensive villas), while its praise of rural ease and simplicity chimes with contemporary philosophical schools such as Epicureanism which sought to inculcate 'freedom from care' and 'the simple life'.

Theocritus' pastoral successors, the 2nd-century BC Greek poets Moschus and Bion, adapted bucolic motifs in their highly polished works, drawing especially on Theocritus' treatment of lamentation and the agonies of love, but it was not until Virgil's *Eclogues*, his first published work, completed in the early to mid-30s BC, that a poet succeeded in taking the genre in a strikingly original and provocative direction. Unlike Theocritus, Virgil created an independent collection of pastoral poems, so here it is the Roman imitation and adaptation of Greek works that crystallizes a genre. Virgil's engagement with the pastoral tradition was clearer in his work's original title, *Bucolica* ('cowherd songs'), which was later replaced by the bland *Eclogues*, meaning 'selections' (from a larger body of texts). Virgil's collection of ten bucolic poems is carefully structured to produce variety (formally or thematically similar poems are separated) but also symmetry. Given the urban focus of the poetry written by Catullus, the most famous Roman poet of the previous generation, Virgil's choice of pastoral may have seemed rather unfashionable, but that was part of its attraction, since he could show his skill and originality by taking on a genre that had never been treated in Latin before and making it relevant to Romans of his time.

Virgil achieved this spectacularly by expanding the boundaries of pastoral to include contemporary politics, and doing so as the whole of the Roman world was mired in civil war. Around the same time (37 BC) the scholar Varro published a prose treatise on farming in dialogue form, *On Rural Matters*, which took a playfully ironic approach to nostalgic, idealizing images of the Roman countryside, but Virgil's choice of pastoral is even more effective, since the destabilizing entry of politics and war into the rural idyll is both poignant and provocative. Thus Virgil revolutionized pastoral, transforming a genre that had been largely apolitical into a profound reflection on the civil war and political violence that were destroying the republic.

After the forces of Antony and Octavian had defeated those of Brutus and Cassius, the assassins of Julius Caesar, at the Battle of Philippi in 42 BC, Octavian's demobilized veterans were settled on confiscated land throughout Italy, leading to forced evictions that had a disastrous effect on rural life. The resulting turmoil is made clear in the *Eclogues'* opening lines, as Meliboeus contrasts his dispossession and painful exile with the luckier fate of his fellow shepherd Tityrus:

> Tityrus, you recline beneath the cover of a spreading beech-tree,
> practising the woodland Muse on your slender pipe;
> we are leaving the borders of our homeland and the fields we love.
> We flee our homeland; you, Tityrus, at ease in the shade,
> are teaching the woods to echo 'Lovely Amaryllis'. (1.1–4)

The mood is even gloomier in *Eclogue* 9, where Moeris must labour on a farm that once belonged to him but is now the property of a distant and unsympathetic soldier. Moeris explains to his friend Lycidas that even their fellow singer, the great Menalcas, has proved unable to save the region with his poetry:

> Our songs, Lycidas,
> have as much power amid the weapons of war
> as they say Chaonian doves have when the eagle swoops. (9.11–13)

The 'eagle' is also the standard of the Roman legions, symbolizing war's destruction of the shepherds' harmonious world. Their songs are not only powerless but are also fading from memory—'now I have forgotten so many songs', laments Moeris (9.53)—and the poem ends with the two waiting for Menalcas, leaving us to wonder when or even if he will ever return.

Like his later works, the *Georgics* and the *Aeneid* (discussed in Chapter 2), the *Eclogues* express a passionate desire for peace, but do so with less confidence, since they pre-date Octavian's definitive emergence as 'restorer of the republic'. Nonetheless, Virgil has opened his collection with a poem which, despite its great sympathy for the dispossessed Meliboeus, also praises a certain 'young man' (i.e. Octavian) for restoring peace and order to the countryside, while the fourth *Eclogue* looks forward to the birth of a child who will herald the return of the Golden Age. The original referent, most likely, was the future son of Antony and Octavia (Octavian's sister), but the hoped for heir was never born and in any case the pact between the two warlords, sealed by the marriage in 40 BC, soon fell apart. It is possible that, to suit the changing times, Virgil revised the poem to express an all-embracing longing for peace and renewal.

While expanding pastoral's political dimension, Virgil also maintains its Theocritean focus on love and the nature and power of poetry itself. Like Theocritus' seventh *Idyll*, the sixth *Eclogue* embodies an Alexandrian aesthetic of small-scale, learned poetry, as Apollo himself urges the poet to 'feed his flock fat, but recite a fine-spun song' (6.4–5). Virgil here adapts a famous scene from Callimachus' *Origins*, and the poem that follows includes the initiation of Virgil's friend Gallus as a poet equal to Callimachus in skill and erudition. And in *Eclogue* 10 Virgil presents Gallus, the great elegiac love poet (see Chapter 3), seeking relief from the cruelty of his mistress Lycoris in the carefree pastoral world of Arcadia, and even trying to give up love elegy for pastoral, but unable in the end to resist his passion, since (his final words) 'Love conquers all, and so let us too yield to Love' (*omnia vincit Amor: et nos cedamus Amori*, 10.69). Virgil thus simultaneously celebrates Gallus' excellence as a love poet while advertising his own command of poetic genre(s). Indeed, a sense of moving on to new 'fields' of poetry is encapsulated in the poem's (and book's) closing lines, where Virgil bids farewell to pastoral, as the singer rises from his bucolic ease beneath the trees and drives his goats home in the falling twilight: 'Go home now with your bellies full, my goats, the evening star is rising, go on, go on' (10.77).

But Virgil did not really leave pastoral behind, since pastoral motifs pervade both the *Georgics* and *Aeneid*, especially their traumatic images of the Italian countryside destroyed by civil war, just as they influence Augustan literature more generally, since Augustus emphasized the reinvigoration of rural life throughout Italy and the empire as one of his many achievements. The few surviving works by Virgil's ancient successors in pastoral lack the subtlety of his political and literary landscape, as their shepherds pipe feel-good panegyrics of the emperor. The poet's distance from the pastoral idyll, and the gap between 'Arcadia' (mentioned only

7. Pastoral in the landscape of British Romanticism: William Blake, 'With Songs the Jovial Hinds Return from Plow', one of a series of woodcut engravings illustrating *The Pastorals of Virgil*, ed. Robert J. Thornton (London, 1821)

occasionally by Virgil, but later *the* symbol of bucolic ease) and messy, less-than-ideal reality, is fundamental to the success of Theocritus and Virgil's versions of pastoral, and its absence led to the syrupyness of much later literature and art in the bucolic tradition. The most successful modern works of pastoral are those that use the gap critically—for example, Milton's condemnation of church corruption in his pastoral elegy *Lycidas* (1638)—and such works show that, in the words of a contemporary poet famous for his use of the form, pastoral is still capable of alerting its audience to 'the ill fit that prevails between the beautifully tinted literary map and the uglier shape that reality has taken in the world' (Seamus Heaney, 'Eclogues *in extremis*: On the Staying Power of Pastoral'; see also Figure 7).

Chapter 8
Satire

This chapter will trace the development of Roman satire from
Lucilius in the 2nd century BC to Juvenal in the early 2nd century
AD, showing how the targets of satire, and the personae adopted
to attack them, reflect changing social and political contexts
(for freedom of speech, for example) in republican and imperial
Rome. We will also consider how the narrative of decline, so
popular in Roman thinking (see Chapter 5), contributes to the
satirists' themes, and examine to what extent their criticisms of
Roman society and literature reinforce cultural norms or
challenge them.

Of all the literary genres discussed in this book, satire is the one
where the debt of Roman authors to Greek predecessors is least
pervasive: as the Roman teacher of rhetoric Quintilian famously
boasted, 'Satire, at any rate, is completely our own' (*Education of
the Orator*, 10.1.93). That is, strictly speaking, a tendentious
claim insofar as it ignores the influence of Greek traditions,
especially those of iambic invective poetry (discussed in
Chapter 3) and the personal and political abuse of Old Comedy
(Chapter 4), on the development of Roman satire. Nonetheless,
Quintilian is partly and importantly justified in the sense that
there was no Greek equivalent to Roman verse satire, and so
although he obscures the fact that satire was influenced by and
incorporated elements from earlier Greek forms of literature, his

statement rightly underlines the distinctiveness of Roman satire and Roman pride in its creation.

The heterogeneous roots of Roman satire, its mixture of forms (both prose and verse), and its varied content (ranging from erudite literary parody to the most vulgar abuse), are all suggested by the name 'satire' itself, which comes from *satura*, meaning 'stuffed sausage', and so promises a literary form that will be crammed full of different ingredients. As we shall see, the satires (especially those of Juvenal) are stuffed full of different tones, themes, and personalities, and they also deal with ideas of over-consumption of all kinds, with greed, gluttony, and desire for excessive wealth and luxury. (In satire, you are what you eat, but with a moral twist.) And insofar as *satura* was a distinctively Roman dish, the name also suggests the national pride displayed by Quintilian in his insistence on Roman originality.

Although Ennius (239–169 BC) wrote the first works called 'satires' (only a few lines survive), the title refers rather to their 'miscellaneous' form and content, and it was Lucilius, writing a generation later, who was considered by the Romans to be the true inventor of satire, and who shaped the genre as a form of poetry characterized by personal invective and social criticism. Of 30 books only 1,300 or so lines survive, but it's enough to see why Lucilius was so influential. He makes use of a powerful poetic persona: the 'I' figure constantly asserts itself and talks about its own experiences and views. And he can make fun of himself too, always a plus in a satirist, since it makes him less distant and censorious: thus someone says, 'we hear he has invited some friends including that reprobate Lucilius' (fr. 929). He also established the social repertoire of the genre: he is interested in morality, and he attacks individuals for moral faults. As well as politics and society, he deals with issues which would have been of interest to aristocratic Romans of his day: philosophy, literature, friendship, even how to spell correctly, and (in a passage reminiscent of the elder Cato: see Chapters 1 and 6) he mocks pretentious Romans who use Greek words when Latin ones will do: 'Furthermore, we solemnly said "*les pieds de divan*" and "*les lampes*"/instead of just "couch legs" and "lamps"' (frs. 15–16).

Lucilius was also responsible for making the hexameter the metre of satire, though he experimented with a range of other metres before finally settling on it. The hexameter was previously associated with epic, so this was a deliberately playful and subversive thing to do, since he was taking the metre associated with the highest form of poetry, epics dealing with the gods and with the deeds of the greatest heroes, and using it in a genre that is interested in the abusive, the mundane, and the least salubrious aspects of human life. For later Romans, especially satirists, Lucilius also embodied the principle of *libertas*, that is, the freedom to criticize powerful men of his own time. This was as much due to his own standing (his family were wealthy and of senatorial status) and his powerful patrons as it was to republican liberty, but later satirists, writing in more troubled or oppressive times, all acknowledge their inability to be so outspoken.

There is a parallel to Lucilius' freedom of speech in Catullus' attacks on contemporary politicians such as Caesar in the 60s–50s BC (Chapter 3). But unlike Lucilius and Catullus, Horace, the next major Roman satirist, writing in the chaotic 30s BC, lacked both high social status and an atmosphere of free public debate. Horace contrasts his own situation with Lucilius' freer age, but his yearning for republican freedom is understandably muted, and he prefers to leave politics to the experts, a form of quietism that can seem rather anaemic when compared to Lucilius and Catullus. However, it is facile to carp at Horace for adapting to new political conditions, and more interesting to see how he turns the more restrained parameters of satire into a positive. Thus Horace explicitly distinguishes his style of satire from that of Lucilius, claiming that his great predecessor's poetry is actually verbose and unpolished, while his own will be concise and elegant:

Yes, I did say that Lucilius' verses did not run smoothly.
Who's so foolish a fan of Lucilius
that he won't admit this? (Horace, *Satires* 1.10.1–3)

Horace emphasizes decorum rather than vulgarity and abuse; his *Satires* are still humorous and moralistic, but in a gentler and more self-deprecating way, with much less obvious aggression. Echoing Lucilius' attacks on luxury and decadence, Horace's *Satires* aim to teach the benefits of moderation and self-sufficiency, but do so in a more measured fashion.

Persius, the third of the great Roman satirists, who wrote under the emperor Nero (50s to early 60s AD), adopts Lucilius' outraged persona, and presents himself as an angry young man who rejects contemporary society and its values. As befits any young rebel worth his salt, he also apears as a student who wakes up late with a hangover (*Satire* 3). In difficult, compressed language Persius illustrates the benefits of philosophical enlightenment over the empty show of imperial politics or the contemporary literary scene, debunking the cliché of poetic inspiration by declaring in his Prologue that poets today are just in it for the money:

If there's even a glimmer of deceitful cash,
you'd think crow-poets and magpie-poetesses
were hymning the nectar of Pegasus. (12–14)

In contrast to Horace's easy-going persona, Persius is stern and unforgiving, and his anger is outdone only by the greatest of Roman satirists, Juvenal, who wrote his five books of *Satires* (16 poems in all) in the early decades of the 2nd century AD.

Juvenal's pose, as a satirist, is that of telling it like it is, cutting through all the lies and hypocrisy and telling the truth, the more shocking and unsavoury the better. Yet he too, like Horace and Persius, dare not attack contemporary public figures: his targets instead are either stereotypical outsiders (foreigners, criminals, etc.) or people from the past, especially from the reign of the emperor Domitian (AD 81–96), now safely dead and the last of his dynasty, who was also a bogeyman for the historian Tacitus (Chapter 5) and other writers of the early 2nd century AD such as Pliny (see Chapter 6 on his *Panegyric*). In his opening *Satire* Juvenal sets himself up as a Lucilius figure, an angry warrior who's going to attack what he needs to, regardless of the risks, only to undercut this image at the end of the poem, where he admits that he's going to take the safe strategy and only attack dead people:

> 'So turn it over in your mind before the bugles sound;
> once your helmet is on, it's too late for second thoughts about
>   combat.'
> Then I'll see what I can get away with saying against those
> whose ashes are buried beneath the Flaminian and the Latin roads.
>
> (1.168–71)

This is oddly anti-climactic, but deliberately so, since it not only parodies the tendency of contemporary writers to rage about the past, but also, by presenting figures from the past as current threats, suggests that past and present are in fact deeply interconnected. In other words, the political past is not simply a safe target because everyone's dead, but rather it and its failings are the route to understanding society's current problems.

Juvenal is undoubtedly the most important figure in the development of satire, since it was his works (especially *Satires* 1–6), with their focus on moral and political corruption and the simultaneous hypocrisy of moralizers and politicians, that did most to shape modern ideas and expectations of satire as a genre. In short, it is thanks to Juvenal that we think of satire as above all political (in the broadest sense), angry, and funny. The comic potential of Juvenal's indignant persona is already clear in *Satire*

1, where he feigns to make anger the very source of his poetry: 'if natural talent is lacking, then indignation will generate my verse' (1.79). Much of the subject matter of Juvenal's satires is familiar from what's come before. The satirists deal with social and moral values, either by advising how one ought to live or by attacking people who in their view get it wrong. This isn't limited to the narrowly political: thus, for example, Juvenal's analysis of the corruption of Rome and of city-life in *Satire* 3, or of women and family life in *Satire* 6, draws on moral, social, and philosophical elements found in Lucilius, Horace, and Persius.

The targets of Juvenal's *Satires* create a moral stance that is clearly conservative: he and his narrators dislike the influx of upstart foreigners and want more respect for poor but freeborn Roman citizens:

> Is that Greek
> going to sign ahead of me and recline on a couch superior to mine
> —a man blown to Rome on the wind that brings us plums and figs?
> Does it count for nothing at all that I, from earliest childhood,
> breathed the Aventine air and was nurtured on the Sabine berry?
>
> (3.81–5)

Juvenal deplores what he sees as the breakdown in the bond between patron and client, one of the cornerstones of Roman society:

> Weary old clients leave the porches
> and abandon their wishes—although nothing lasts so long with a
> man
> as the hope of a dinner. The poor sods have got to buy their cabbage
> and kindling.
> Meanwhile, his lordship will be chomping his way through the
> finest produce of forest and sea,
> lying alone among empty couches. (1.132–6)

And his narrators are troubled by social mobility and the idea that the sorts of people who now become *equites* ('knights') aren't what they used to be:

> 'If you have any sense of shame,' someone says,
> 'please stand up and leave the cushioned seats reserved for the
>   knights,
> if your wealth is less than the law requires. Your place will be taken
> by the sons of pimps, born in whatever whorehouse.
> The slick son of an auctioneer may sit and applaud here
> alongside the well-dressed lads of a gladiator or a trainer.'

> (3.153–8)

Nor does he approve of modern decadence, whether that's the homosexuals of *Satire* 2, the loose women of *Satire* 6, or the overlavish banquets of *Satires* 4 and 5. So the moral outlook of Juvenal's *Satires* is fairly consistent: he regards modern society as debauched and corrupt, and he takes the side of the poor but freeborn Roman citizen, often someone whose family has come down in the world.

On this description, Juvenal doesn't sound particularly funny at all—in fact, he sounds rather like a *Daily Mail* editorial: reactionary, moralistic, and bombastic. But this description passes over a lot of the subtleties in the way Juvenal actually couches these attacks—for Juvenal regularly sets up situations that cause us to question the reality or sincerity of the attacks being made, and so leaves us unsure who we're meant to be laughing at. In *Satire* 3, for example, we're led to question the reliability of the narrator, Juvenal's friend Umbricius (whose name, significantly, means 'Mr Shady'), who is leaving Rome in disgust. After a long list of complaints about the Greeks' immorality and particularly their abilities at flattery, Umbricius concludes:

> There's no place for a Roman here, where some
> Protogenes or Diphilus or Hermarchus is king.

A man like that never shares a friend (it's a defect of his race),
but keeps him for himself. For once he's dripped into his patron's
      ready ear
a drop of the poison that comes naturally to him and his country,
I am hustled away from the doorstep, and wasted are my long years
of slavery. Nowhere is it less of a big deal to ditch a client.

(3.119–25)

But what Umbricius is complaining about isn't that Greeks are
lying flatterers per se, it's that they're better at it than he is. In
other words, Umbricius complains that he was perfectly happy
spending his time in 'slavery' (i.e. flattery and service) to a rich
man until the Greeks outclassed him with their gift for words, and
so made his offices redundant. Far from being a guardian of good
old-fashioned Roman values, Umbricius is revealed as something
of a hypocrite, who's simply envious and bitter at losing his own
position, and so attacks foreigners for the very quality he envies
their success at.

We can see a similarly alienating effect in the excess with which
Juvenal's own angry personae attack their targets. *Satire* 6, for
example, Juvenal's diatribe against women, is undone by its sheer
sensationalism. The two women Tullia and Maura aren't just
portrayed as adulterous or deceitful (standard complaints of
misogynistic poetry), but instead Juvenal conjures up the
grotesque image of them literally pissing on the altar of Chastity
and then having lesbian sex in their own urine (6.309–13). Such
passages make us laugh as much at the satirical persona himself
for the absurd views he espouses as we do at the targets of his
abuse.

So in Juvenal's *Satires* the arbiters of morality are frequently
exposed as hypocrites or as absurd, excessive characters in their
own right. The narrator is hilarious but also repellent at the same
time, creating an unsettling effect, whereby we feel uncomfortable
at laughing along with him. We might compare modern

comedians who deal with controversial topics in an edgy or deliberately offensive way, so that we, the audience, feel rather uneasy about laughing at their jokes. Juvenal's *Satires* thus work on more than one level: the naïve reader may see his beliefs and prejudices confirmed, especially where the targets are easy ones (the corrupt or parasitic) or marginal groups (foreigners, homosexuals, women). Or he may identify with Juvenal's Everyman persona, especially in his defence of the honest and decent Roman who's worried about his place in society. But the outraged moralist often emerges as no better than the people he criticizes. Juvenal's unreliable narrator is thus a challenge to the reader to recognize his or her own self-deception and hypocrisy. Jonathan Swift famously said that 'Satire is a sort of glass wherein beholders do generally discover everybody's face but their own' (Preface to *The Battle of the Books*, 1704), and Juvenal's constant shifting of the targets of satire shows that we should be careful who we mock, in case we find ourselves equally open to abuse.

Finally, we must remember not to be too po-faced about Juvenal, or any other comic writer, since he's out to entertain as much as critique society (as are modern political comedians), and his wit and comic timing are brilliant. Let one last example suffice, from *Satire* 3 on the perils of life in the big city (the model for Samuel Johnson's *London*, 1738):

> Have you ever seen a place so dismal, so lonely
> that it doesn't seem worse to live in constant dread of fires,
> buildings collapsing suddenly, the thousand other dangers of
>   savage Rome—
> not to mention poets reciting their work in the month of August?
>
> (3.6–9)

Chapter 9
Novel

This final chapter will discuss the ancient novel, a relative
latecomer to Greek and Latin literature, but a testament to the
innovation and dynamism that characterize the classical tradition
throughout. Starting with the five surviving examples of the Greek
novel, dating from the mid-1st century AD onwards, we will
consider the popular appeal of their typical motifs of love and
adventure, and see their increasingly sophisticated narrative
techniques. The chapter will also examine how the social and
political values embodied in these Greek prose fictions related to
those of their audiences, both Greek and Roman, under Roman
imperial rule. As we'll see, the manipulation and parody of generic
convention found in the Greek novels is even more central to the
Latin novels of Petronius and Apuleius, whose works well
illustrate (yet again) the crucial ability of Roman authors to recast
the literary tradition in a distinctively Roman way.

Though our focus is on the Greek and Roman novel, it should be
stressed that there were many different kinds of prose fiction in
antiquity—from fictional letters and biographies to tales of
utopian or fantastic travel. Thus the capacity of fictional prose
narrative to take many forms in the modern world (from detective
novel to romance, from historical novel to science fiction, and so
on) continues a feature of classical literature. Ancient readers had

no specific name for the novel as a genre, since it developed after the formative period of genre classification in Hellenistic Alexandria (see Chapter 1). But despite the lack of an ancient name, we can still see family resemblances and established conventions in the surviving texts, and modern scholars reserve the term 'novel' for these seven works of prose fiction—five Greek, two Latin—distinguishing between the romantic focus of the Greek novels and the comic-realist style of the Latin.

The ancient Greek novel, like the modern European novel from *Don Quixote* (1605–15) onwards, was an omnivorous genre, incorporating elements from many different literary forms, including epic (especially Homer's *Odyssey*, with its tales of exotic adventure) and drama (particularly the thwarted yet happy-ever-after love affairs of New Comedy), but also adapting influences from Egyptian and Near Eastern cultures. With the exception of Longus' pastoral idyll, *Daphnis and Chloe*, the surviving texts display a number of typical plot features whereby a well-born boy and girl fall in love, but are then separated and exposed to various dangers before finally being reunited. The main themes of the genre are well summed up by a passage from the earliest example, Chariton's *Callirhoe* (mid-1st century AD), where the narrator, in the preface to the eighth and final book, promises his readers a happy ending:

> I think that this final book will be particularly pleasurable for my readers, for it brings relief from the distressing things in the earlier ones. No longer will there be piracy or slavery or lawsuits or fighting or suicide or war or captivity, but rightful love and lawful marriage. (8.1)

It would be a mistake to dismiss such plots as formulaic, however, since ancient audiences clearly enjoyed such patterns (as do readers of modern genre fiction), while the interest and skill of each work lies in part in its ability to ring the changes on the genre's familiar and popular themes: love at first sight, kidnap by pirates, storms and shipwrecks, imprisonment, threats to both life and chastity, last-minute recognition, and married bliss.

Chariton's 'Dear reader' technique in *Callirhoe* reminds us that self-conscious play with the audience's literary expectations is a feature of the genre right from the start—an important point, since the Greek—and Roman—novel's literary sophistication suggests an educated readership. (Ancient critics ignored the novel as an 'inferior' genre, but that didn't dent its popularity with readers. One might compare the modern reader who enjoys both 'critically acclaimed' works and the latest bestseller or pulp-fiction.) In Xenophon's *Anthia and Habrocomes* (early to mid-2nd century AD) we get a fast-paced action thriller, with one suspense-filled episode after another, as when the heroine is buried alive but then 'rescued' by robbers breaking into her tomb in search of treasure. In Achilles Tatius' *Leucippe and Clitophon* (second half of the 2nd century AD) the story is told by Clitophon himself to the writer, the only example of first-person narrative in the Greek novels (the others are in the third person), which cleverly creates irony and tension since we share the protagonist's limited view of events, as when he (and we) believe that Leucippe has been murdered but she turns out to be fine—though the fact that Achilles uses such a scene three times suggests that he's poking fun at the plot device of apparent death used in other novels.

Longus' *Daphnis and Chloe* (late 2nd or early 3rd century AD) fuses the romantic novel with Theocritean pastoral poetry (Chapter 7), as the young protagonists meet and fall in love as shepherds on the island of Lesbos, and even though they eventually discover that they are the offspring of wealthy urbanites, they return from their taste of the Big City to marry and raise a family in their bucolic paradise. In the latest and longest of the Greek novels, Heliodorus' *Charicleia and Theagenes* (ten books, 3rd or 4th century AD), the narrative is handled with particular virtuosity. Heliodorus plunges the reader *in medias res*, as the novel opens with a striking and mysterious scene—an Egyptian beach strewn with bodies and booty, a beautiful female survivor caring for her wounded male companion—and it is only after several books of exciting back story (as in Homer's *Odyssey*) that we understand how the protagonists got into such a pickle.

Like their modern counterparts, ancient novels offer their readers a world where they can escape and be entertained, but the nature of these fictional Greek worlds is revealing: the scene is usually the classical past, for example, and there are no Romans anywhere, even when the setting is that of the empire. So, like the fantasy and utopian worlds of Greek Old Comedy (Chapter 4), the 'escapism' of the novels is culturally and politically charged, keying into Greek nostalgia for a time of political independence—shared by 'Greek' (in the sense of Greek-speaking) communities throughout the empire, whether Egyptian, Syrian, Jewish... —and Roman admiration for Greece's cultural heritage.

The novels' focus on idealized romantic love is also significant for what it reveals about sexual politics: heroines should remain virgins until marriage, their male beloveds occasionally succumb to temptation. In Longus' *Daphnis and Chloe*, we witness the sexual education of the naïve young shepherds (Daphnis is 15, Chloe 13), including Daphnis' sexual initiation by an older married woman from the city, and there is both humour and voyeurism in the teenagers' failed attempts to make love 'as the rams do to the ewes and the billy-goats to the nannies' (3.14). The pastoral 'innocence' of the countryside is matched by that of the rustic protagonists (again, more urban fantasy: see Chapter 7). As in the early English novel, the Greek novel plot typically revolves around marriage, and it is often the clever and spirited heroines who impress the reader more and guide the plot to its cheerful conclusion. Men still end up on top, but they are punished when they dishonour respectable women, as in Chariton's *Callirhoe*, for example, where the jealous Chaereas kicks his pregnant wife, thinks he's killed her, and ends up a slave (but don't worry: they all live happily ever after ...).

The major Roman novels that survive, the *Satyrica* of Petronius (*c*.50s–60s AD) and the *Metamorphoses* or *Golden Ass* of Apuleius (*c*.AD 150–180), assume a readership familiar with what would become the typical story-patterns of the Greek romantic novel, but each takes the genre in a distinctively original direction. Petronius is very likely the politician and 'Arbiter of Taste' (*elegentiae arbiter*, as Tacitus styles him) at Nero's court, who was forced to commit suicide in AD 66 when Nero's henchman Tigellinus grew jealous of his influence and denounced him. Tacitus describes how this Petronius refused to die in the Stoic manner, but spent his last hours listening to frivolous poetry and then exposed details of Nero's debauchery in his will (*Annals* 16.18–19). In any case, a similarly irreverent and parodic spirit is evident in the *Satyrica*, which draws on the many forms of literature being written in the Neronian period (including epic, tragedy, philosophical treatises, and satire) to create a novel that is both an ingenious generic collage and a hilariously mordant critique of contemporary Roman society.

Petronius' novel was originally very long (perhaps 20 books) but survives only in fragments. These are, nonetheless, full of incident and depict the picaresque adventures of Encolpius, who is also the narrator, as he travels around the fashionable bay of Naples and the sleazier parts of southern Italy with his (unfaithful) boyfriend Giton in search of *la dolce vita* and a free dinner. Petronius' parody of romantic plot conventions is a technique repeated in the early stages of the English novel: Henry Fielding's *Joseph Andrews* (1742), for example, advertises itself as a 'comic romance' and begins as a parody of Samuel Richardson's *Pamela* (1740). Debates about rhetoric, poetic recitations, lovers' tiffs, bisexual orgies—there is something for every taste in the *Satyrica*'s free-wheeling narrative (see Figure 8).

8. Wall-painting from a brothel at Pompeii with young man and prostitute (first century AD). Petronius' narrator frequents such establishments as often as he can

The raunchy subject matter is flagged by the title, 'Tale of the Satyrs', evoking the bestial and perennially horny creatures of Greek myth. Like the satyrs, Encolpius and his friends live for the moment and are slaves to sensual pleasure. But the satyric thrust is also comically deflated, when Encolpius (whose name fits: 'Mr In-the-Crotch') can't get it up, despite the attentions of a gorgeous nymphomaniac ('Circe', evoking the seductress from Homer's *Odyssey*), prompting him to threaten his own penis with castration and to address it in mock-heroic anger—'Is this what I have deserved of you, that when I am in heaven you should drag me down to hell?' (132) Later Encolpius blames his impotence on the 'terrible anger' of the phallic god Priapus (139), parodying the hostile gods of epic. Similarly, in an earlier scene aboard the ship of Lichas ('Captain Blowjob'), the disguised Encolpius is recognized by his genitals, a discovery which he himself compares to the famous scene from Homer's *Odyssey* where the hero is recognized by a hunting scar (105). Penises aside, the title *Satyrica* also alludes to the Roman genre of satire (*satura*), whose irreverent influence is evident in many episodes, especially the overblown and tasteless banquet hosted by Trimalchio, to which Encolpius and his friends secure an invitation.

Trimalchio's Dinner-Party, the longest surviving episode of the novel, is a *tour de force* of class comedy and social satire. Trimalchio, an ex-slave and self-made millionaire, seeks to impress by serving a fantastic array of dishes, but his gross display of wealth is matched only by his ignorance of culture and etiquette, as he garbles Greek mythology—'I own a bowl where Daedalus is shown shutting Niobe up in the Trojan Horse' (52)—and lectures his guests on the dangers of holding in their farts:

> 'Believe me, the rising vapours attack the brain and surge through
> the whole body. I know a lot of people have died that way because
> they wouldn't be honest with themselves.' We thanked him for being
> so generous and considerate and promptly tried to suppress our
> laughter by taking frequent swigs of wine. (47)

Encolpius the narrator's contempt for the vulgarity of the *nouveau riche* Trimalchio reflects contemporary Roman anxieties about the social mobility of ex-slaves, but the reader is not simply encouraged to sneer at Trimalchio, since the snobbery of Encolpius (himself a thief and a sponger) is also satirized. The episode thus presents a biting and hilarious critique of materialism, wealth, and class in contemporary Rome, not only lampooning the corruption and decadence of Neronian society, where all are scrabbling for money, sex, and power, but also skewering the pretensions of those who, like the hypocritical Greek Encolpius, assume an air of moral or social superiority. Thus the *Satyrica*, like many great comic novels since, is also a masterpiece of penetrating social analysis.

The literary range and virtuosity of Petronius' *Satyrica* is matched by that of Apuleius' novel, whose original title was *Metamorphoses*, though it is more popularly known as *The Golden*

123

Ass (the name given to it by St Augustine: *City of God*, 18.18). Apuleius was born around AD 125 in Madaurus (in modern Algeria), and his ambitious work (11 books) is the only Roman novel to have survived complete. The narrator, a Greek called Lucius, tells how he was accidentally transformed into an ass while prying into the secrets of magic. He then recounts his frequently bawdy adventures (and many others that he hears of with his big ass-ears) as he is passed from one dodgy owner to the next, until he finally returns to human form thanks to the goddess Isis and converts to her cult. Among the many tales inserted into the main plot the lengthiest and most famous is that of Cupid and Psyche (4.28–6.24), where Psyche's curiosity (to see her divine lover) leads to much wandering and suffering only ended by divine intervention—paralleling the story of Lucius himself.

As with Encolpius in the *Satyrica*, the reactions of Lucius/the ass, who is often shocked or bewildered by what is happening to him, generate a great deal of comedy, and the *Metamorphoses'* combination of saucy and philosophical-mystical elements is one of its most original and entertaining features. Thus, for example, when a rich woman sees Lucius/the ass performing tricks in a travelling sideshow, she takes a fancy to him and has sex with him, giving his owner the bright idea that the ass should do the same with a condemned female prisoner in the arena before a paying public. But Lucius runs away and prays to the Queen of Heaven, who appears to him as Isis and instructs him both how to regain his human form (by eating roses scattered the next day in a procession in her honour) and to dedicate his life to her.

The narrator's unconventional journey to enlightenment and salvation is given a final twist, however, as Lucius is revealed to be Apuleius himself (11.27), a brilliant literary metamorphosis of narrator into author, which plays with the very act of writing fiction, where the author creates the identity of the fictional character. (Again, one might compare Fielding's *Joseph Andrews*, where Joseph turns out to be the long-lost son of Mr Wilson, whose life recalls that of Fielding himself.) So this is no earnest pilgrim's progress intended to convert the reader to the mystery cults of Isis and Osiris, and the humorous ending takes us back to the spirit of the novel's Prologue, where we were told: 'Reader, pay attention to the story; you'll enjoy it'. Nonetheless, the *Metamorphoses*' final book points to the genuine interest of 2nd-century AD pagan audiences in cults that promised a release from the bondage of the flesh and a blessed afterlife, and reminds us that another cult of that kind was then rising in the east which would one day span the empire.

Epilogue

Naturally, one can't cover everything worth mentioning about classical literature in a *Very Short Introduction*—or even a very long one—but I have tried to show that this literature is far from being stuffy or irrelevant, and that its best works remain as entertaining and provocative as ever. In my beginning is my end (to quote a modern classic), and so let the last word on the power of literature go to Homer, describing the effects of the bard Demodocus' song about the Greeks' destruction of Troy:

> Thus sang the famous singer; but Odysseus' heart was melted,
> tears dropped from his eyes and soaked his cheeks.
> As a woman weeps, falling to clasp her husband,
> who has fallen in defence of his city and his people,
> to ward off the pitiless day of destruction from his town and his children;
> seeing him gasp in the throes of death,
> she clings to him, shrieking loudly; but the enemy,
> striking her back and shoulders with their spears,
> lead her off into slavery, to have toil and misery;
> and her cheeks are wasted with the most pitiable grief—
> just so did Odysseus drop pitiable tears from his eyes.
>
> (*Odyssey* 8.521–31)

Further reading

This is a highly selective list, limited to books in English; more detailed bibliographies are given in the suggested works, or can be found in the relevant section of S. Hornblower, A. Spawforth, and E. Eidinow, eds., *The Oxford Classical Dictionary*, 4th edn. (Oxford, 2012).

Translations

Excellent and up-to-date translations of the works discussed in this
    book are available in the following series:
The World's Classics (Oxford University Press)
<http://www.oup.co.uk/worldsclassics>
The Penguin Classics (Penguin Books)
<http://www.penguinclassics.co.uk>
Greek and Latin texts with a facing English translation:
The Loeb Classical Library (Harvard University Press)
<http://www.hup.harvard.edu>

Chapter 1: History, genre, text

History of the classical world: S. Price and P. Thonemann, *The Birth of
    Classical Europe: A History from Troy to Augustine* (London,
    2011).
Where it all happened: R. J. A. Talbert, ed., *Atlas of Classical History*
    (London, 1985).

The importance of genre: A. Fowler, *Kinds of Literature: An Introduction to the Theory of Genres and Modes* (Oxford, 1982).

Ancient critics on their own literature: D. A. Russell and M. Winterbottom, eds., *Classical Literary Criticism* (Oxford, 1989).

The transmission of classical texts: L. D. Reynolds and N. G. Wilson, *Scribes and Scholars: A Guide to the Transmission of Greek and Latin Literature*, 3rd edn. (Oxford, 1991).

The impact of Christianity: R. Lane Fox, *Pagans and Christians* (London, 1986).

New papyrological discoveries: P. Parsons, *City of the Sharp-Nosed Fish: Greek Lives in Roman Egypt* (London, 2007).

Chapter 2: Epic

The genre: J. B. Hainsworth, *The Idea of Epic* (Berkeley, 1991).

Homer's *Iliad*: W. Allan, *Homer: The Iliad* (London, 2012).

Homer's *Odyssey*: J. Griffin, *Homer: The Odyssey*, 2nd edn. (Cambridge, 2004).

Hellenistic variations: R. L. Hunter, *The Argonautica of Apollonius: Literary Studies* (Cambridge, 1993).

Early Latin epic: S. M. Goldberg, *Epic in Republican Rome* (Oxford, 1995).

Virgil's *Aeneid*: K. W. Gransden, *Virgil: The Aeneid*, 2nd edn. (Cambridge, 2004).

Ovid's transformation of epic: E. Fantham, *Ovid's Metamorphoses* (Oxford, 2004).

Lucan and civil war: J. Masters, *Poetry and Civil War in Lucan's Bellum Civile* (Cambridge, 1992).

Hesiod's dour picture of the world: J. S. Clay, *Hesiod's Cosmos* (Cambridge, 2003).

Lucretius' Epicurean universe: D. Sedley, *Lucretius and the Transformation of Greek Wisdom* (Cambridge, 1998).

The poetry and politics of Virgil's *Georgics*: L. Morgan, *Patterns of Redemption in Virgil's Georgics* (Cambridge, 1999).

Chapter 3: Lyric and personal poetry

Greek lyric poetry: D. E. Gerber, ed., *A Companion to the Greek Lyric Poets* (Leiden, 1997).

Wine, song, sex, politics: O. Murray, ed., *Sympotica: A Symposium on the Symposion* (Oxford, 1990).

Pindar and his patrons: L. Kurke, *The Traffic in Praise: Pindar and the Poetics of Social Economy* (Ithaca, NY, 1991).

Catullus and Roman society: T. P. Wiseman, *Catullus and His World: A Reappraisal* (Cambridge, 1985).

Latin love elegy: P. Veyne, *Roman Erotic Elegy: Love, Poetry, and the West*, trans. D. Pellauer (Chicago, 1988).

Horace and Augustan literature: P. White, *Promised Verse: Poets in the Society of Augustan Rome* (Cambridge, MA, 1993).

Chapter 4: Drama

The roots of Greek tragedy: J. Herington, *Poetry into Drama: Early Tragedy and the Greek Poetic Tradition* (Berkeley, 1985).

The variety of tragedy: R. Scodel, *An Introduction to Greek Tragedy* (Cambridge, 2010).

The importance of choral song and dance: L. A. Swift, *The Hidden Chorus: Echoes of Genre in Tragic Lyric* (Oxford, 2010).

Athenian life and politics in Aristophanic comedy: D. M. MacDowell, *Aristophanes and Athens: An Introduction to the Plays* (Oxford, 1995).

New Comedy: R. L. Hunter, *The New Comedy of Greece and Rome* (Cambridge, 1985).

Seneca's transformation of tragedy: A. J. Boyle, *Roman Tragedy* (London, 2006).

Chapter 5: Historiography

Herodotus' achievement: J. Gould, *Herodotus* (London, 1989).

Thucydides' understanding of war: W. R. Connor, *Thucydides* (Princeton, 1984).

History as literature/literature as history: C. Pelling, *Literary Texts and the Greek Historian* (London, 2000).

Polybius and Rome: F. W. Walbank, *Polybius* (Berkeley, 1972).

Sallust and the politics of the republic: R. Syme, *Sallust* (Berkeley, 1964).

Caesar's self-presentation: K. Welch and A. Powell, eds., *Julius Caesar as Artful Reporter: The War Commentaries as Political Instruments* (London, 1998).

Livy and the Roman past: J. D. Chaplin, *Livy's Exemplary History* (Oxford, 2000).

Tacitus and the imperial system: R. Syme, *Tacitus*, 2 vols. (Oxford, 1958).

Classical historiography and later Western thought: A. Momigliano, *The Classical Foundations of Modern Historiography* (Berkeley, 1990).

Chapter 6: Oratory

The origins of rhetoric: E. Schiappa, *The Beginnings of Rhetorical Theory in Classical Greece* (New Haven, 1999).

Democracy and persuasion: J. Hesk, *Deception and Democracy in Classical Athens* (Cambridge, 2000).

Legal contexts: D. M. MacDowell, *The Law in Classical Athens* (London, 1978).

Praising the dead: J. Herrman, *Athenian Funeral Orations* (Newburyport, MA, 2004).

Lysias and Athenian society: C. Carey, *Trials from Classical Athens*, 2nd edn. (London, 2011).

The skill of Demosthenes: D. M. MacDowell, *Demosthenes the Orator* (Oxford, 2009).

Cicero's personae: C. Steel, *Reading Cicero: Genre and Performance in Late Republican Rome* (London, 2005).

The function of praise in the Roman empire: R. Rees, ed., *Latin Panegyric* (Oxford, 2012).

Overcoming prejudice against rhetoric: B. Vickers, *In Defence of Rhetoric* (Oxford, 1998).

Chapter 7: Pastoral

The nature of pastoral: P. Alpers, *What is Pastoral?* (Chicago, 1996).

Urban nostalgia: R. Williams, *The Country and the City* (Oxford, 1973).

The many uses of pastoral: A. Patterson, *Pastoral and Ideology: Virgil to Valéry* (Berkeley, 1987).

Theocritus' bucolic idylls: K. J. Gutzwiller, *Theocritus' Pastoral Analogies: The Formation of a Genre* (Madison, 1991).

Virgil's expansion of the genre: P. Alpers, *The Singer of the Eclogues: A Study of Virgilian Pastoral* (Berkeley, 1979).

Idyllic landscapes in Roman wall-painting: E. Winsor Leach, *Vergil's Eclogues: Landscapes of Experience* (Ithaca, NY, 1974).

Poetry about poetry: G. Williams, *Tradition and Originality in Roman Poetry* (Oxford, 1968).

Chapter 8: Satire

A Roman genre: M. Coffey, *Roman Satire*, 2nd edn. (Bristol, 1989).

The 'threat' of satire: K. Freudenburg, *Satires of Rome: Threatening Poses from Lucilius to Juvenal* (Cambridge, 2001).

Lucilius and Hellenism: E. S. Gruen, *Culture and National Identity in Republican Rome* (Ithaca, NY, 1992), ch. 7.

Catullus as social commentator: C. Nappa, *Aspects of Catullus' Social Fiction* (Frankfurt, 2001).

Horace's satirical persona: W. S. Anderson, *Essays on Roman Satire* (Princeton, 1982).

Decoding Persius: J. C. Bramble, *Persius and the Programmatic Satire: A Study in Form and Imagery* (Cambridge, 1974).

Consumption and decadence: E. Gowers, *The Loaded Table: Representations of Food in Roman Literature* (Oxford, 1993).

Mockery and self-ridicule: M. Plaza, *The Function of Humour in Roman Verse Satire: Laughing and Lying* (Oxford, 2006).

Chapter 9: Novel

The genre in antiquity: N. Holzberg, *The Ancient Novel: An Introduction* (London, 1995).

The Greek novels in translation: B. P. Reardon, ed., *Collected Ancient Greek Novels*, 2nd edn. (Berkeley, 2008).

Greece under Rome: S. Swain, *Hellenism and Empire: Language, Classicism, and Power in the Greek World AD 50–250* (Oxford, 1996).

The novel in Rome: P. G. Walsh, *The Roman Novel: The 'Satyricon' of Petronius and the 'Metamorphoses' of Apuleius* (Cambridge, 1970).

Funny things happen on the way to the forum: J. R. W. Prag and I. D. Repath, eds., *Petronius: A Handbook* (Chichester, 2009).

Being an ass: C. C. Schlam, *The Metamorphoses of Apuleius: On Making an Ass of Oneself* (Chapel Hill, 1992).

Index

Expand your collection of
VERY SHORT INTRODUCTIONS

JOIN OUR COMMUNITY

www.oup.com/vsi

- Join us online at the official Very Short Introductions **Facebook** page.
- Access the thoughts and musings of our authors with our online **blog**.
- Sign up for our monthly **e-newsletter** to receive information on all new titles publishing that month.
- Browse the full range of Very Short Introductions online.
- Read **extracts** from the Introductions for free.
- Visit our library of **Reading Guides**. These guides, written by our expert authors will help you to question again, why you think what you think.
- If you are a teacher or lecturer you can order inspection copies quickly and simply via our website.

Visit the Very Short Introductions website to access all this and more for free.

www.oup.com/vsi

SOCIAL MEDIA
Very Short Introduction

Join our community
www.oup.com/vsi

- Join us online at the official Very Short Introductions **Facebook** page.
- Access the thoughts and musings of our authors with our online **blog**.
- Sign up for our monthly **e-newsletter** to receive information on all new titles publishing that month.
- Browse the full range of Very Short Introductions online.
- Read **extracts** from the Introductions for free.
- Visit our library of **Reading Guides**. These guides, written by our expert authors will help you to question again, why you think what you think.
- If you are a teacher or lecturer you can order inspection copies quickly and simply via our website.

ONLINE CATALOGUE
A Very Short Introduction

Our online catalogue is designed to make it easy to find your ideal Very Short Introduction. View the entire collection by subject area, watch author videos, read sample chapters, and download reading guides.

http://fds.oup.com/www.oup.co.uk/general/vsi/index.html